H. G. WELLS

THE INVISIBLE MAN

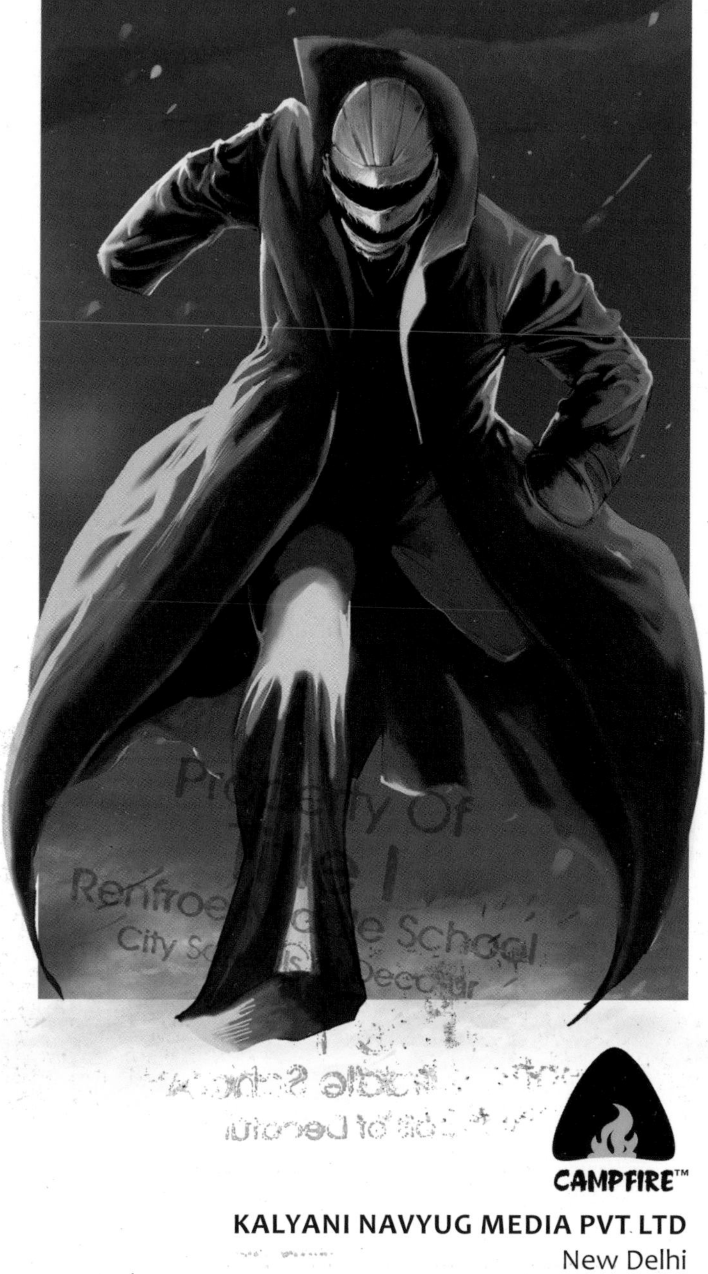

CAMPFIRE™

KALYANI NAVYUG MEDIA PVT. LTD
New Delhi

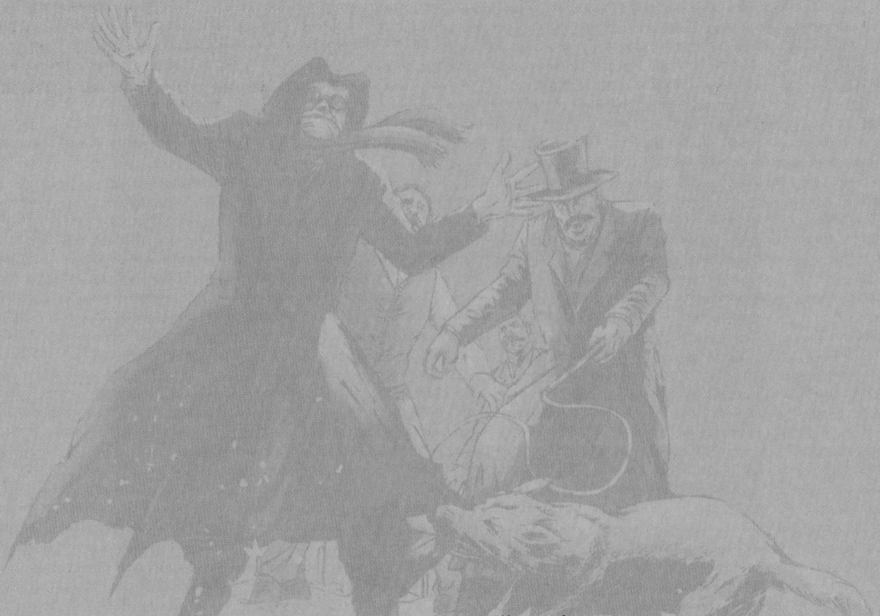

Sitting around the Campfire, telling the story, were:

Wordsmith	:	Sean Taylor
Illustrator	:	Bhupendra Ahluwalia
Illustrations Editor	:	Jayshree Das
Colorist	:	Anil C. K.
Letterers	:	Bhavnath Chaudhary
		Vishal Sharma
Editors	:	Eman Chowdhary
		Divya Dubey
Editor (Information Content)	:	Pushpanjali Borooah
Production Controller	:	Vishal Sharma

Cover Artists:

Illustrator	:	Bhupendra Ahluwalia
Colorist	:	Anil C. K.
Designer	:	Pushpa Verma

Published by Kalyani Navyug Media Pvt Ltd
101 C, Shiv House, Hari Nagar Ashram
New Delhi 110014
India
www.campfire.co.in

ISBN: 978-93-80028-29-3

Printed in India at Tara Art Printers Pvt Ltd.

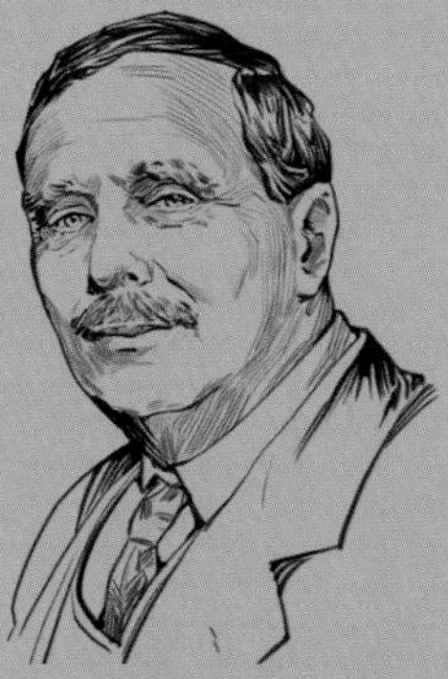

About the Author

Considered one of the pioneers of science fiction, Herbert George Wells was born in England on September 21, 1866. He was the son of domestic servants who later became shopkeepers. Wells always had a great passion for reading but, with his family struggling to make ends meet, he spent much of his youth shuttling between school and a series of odd jobs. He did everything from working as an apprentice to a draper, from acting as an assistant to a chemist.

At the age of 18, Wells joined The Normal School of Science in Kensington to study biology. Here he was taught by T. H. Huxley. This was a crucial period of his life as it had an immense influence on his writing.

Wells received a Bachelor of Science from the University of London in 1888, and began to teach. He enjoyed writing stories and articles alongside his day job, and gradually moved into writing on a full-time basis. He married his cousin, Isabel Mary Wells, in 1891.

A turning point for Wells, both personally and professionally, was in 1895. This was the year he left his first wife and married a former student, Amy Catherine Robbins. It was also the year when his first major novel, *The Time Machine*, was published.

Still considered one of the greatest science fiction novels of all time, *The Time Machine* was the first in a string of successful books in which Wells's unique take on unusual subjects came to define certain genres. His tales of alien invasions in *The War of the Worlds*, invisibility in *The Invisible Man*, and eugenics in *The Island of Doctor Moreau* have influenced generations of writers.

While most famous for his work in science fiction, Wells worked on a variety of genres. An advocate of social change and a member of the British socialist group, the Fabian Society, Wells spent much of his later years writing about his views on politics and society, and even offered predictions about the direction in which the world was headed. H. G. Wells continued writing until his death at the age of 79 in 1946.

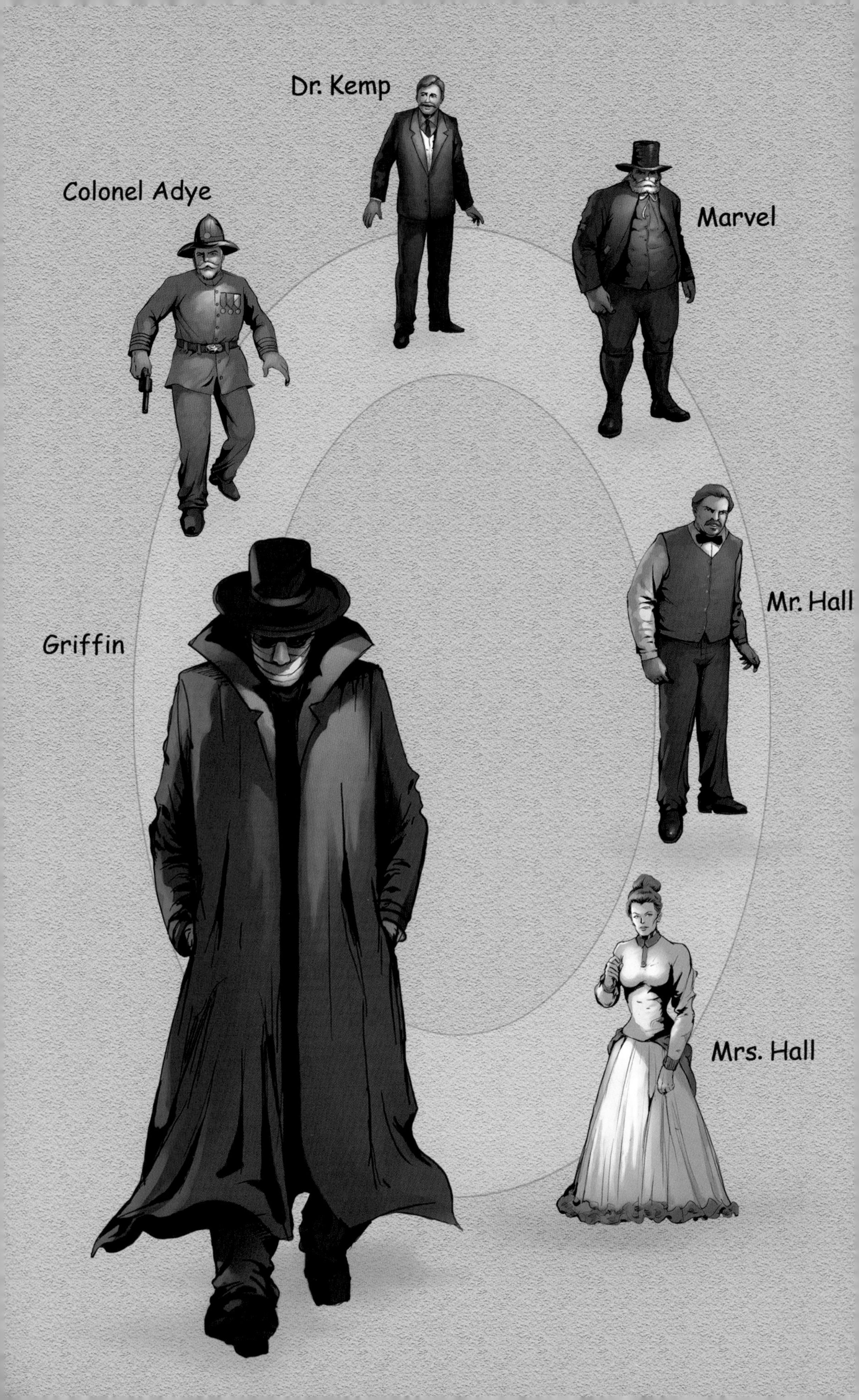
Dr. Kemp
Colonel Adye
Marvel
Mr. Hall
Griffin
Mrs. Hall

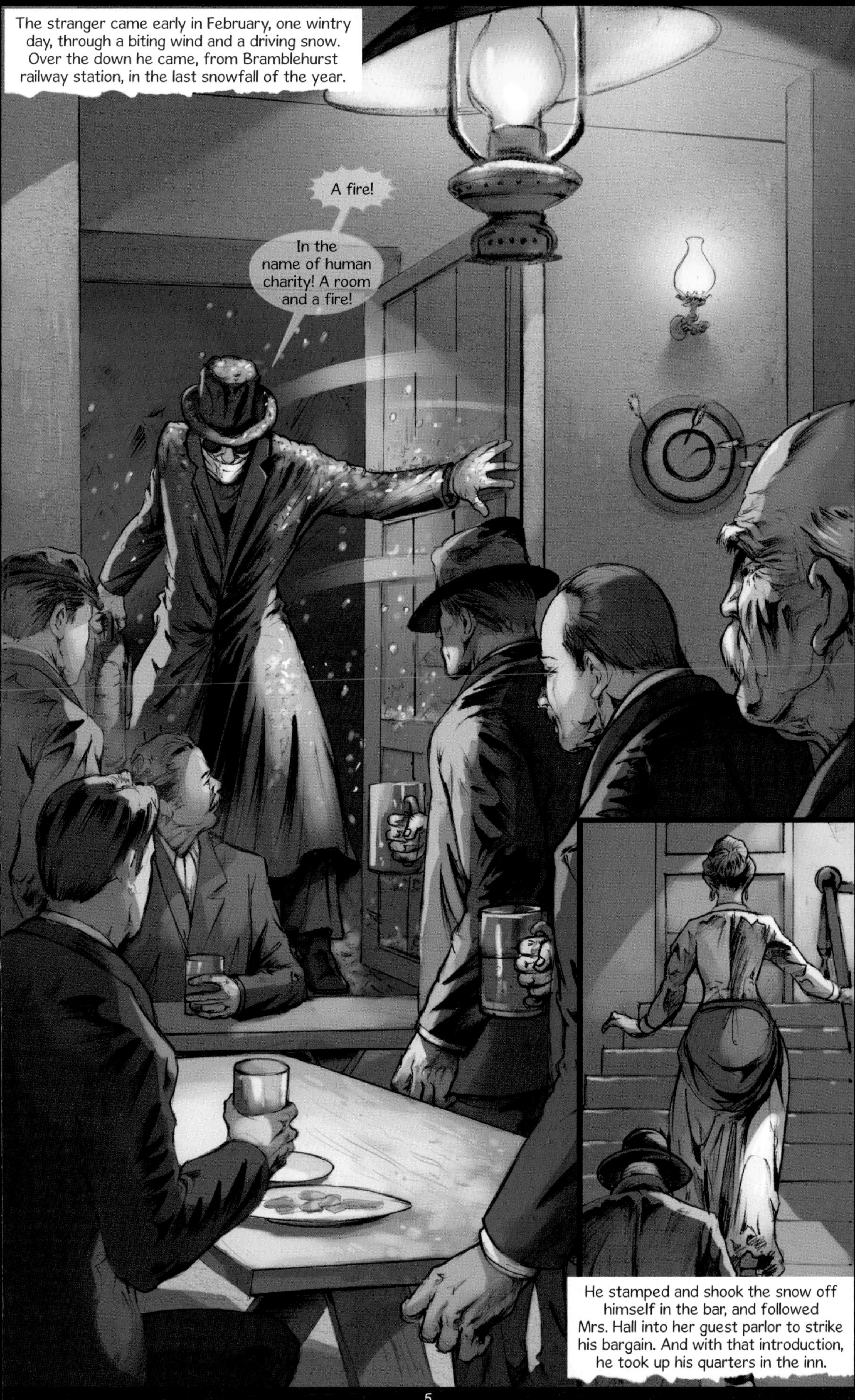

The stranger came early in February, one wintry day, through a biting wind and a driving snow. Over the down he came, from Bramblehurst railway station, in the last snowfall of the year.
A fire!
In the name of human charity! A room and a fire!
He stamped and shook the snow off himself in the bar, and followed Mrs. Hall into her guest parlor to strike his bargain. And with that introduction, he took up his quarters in the inn.

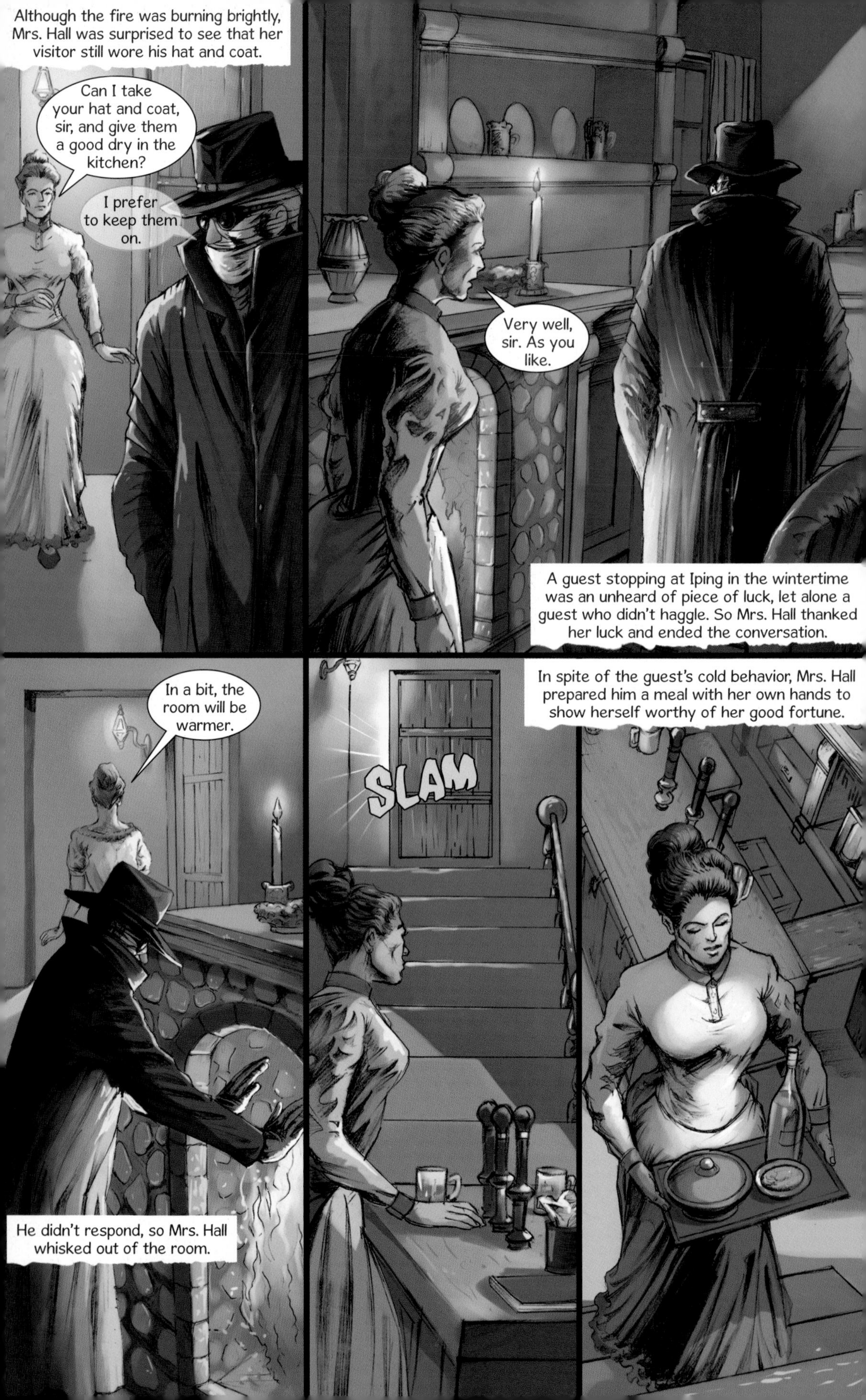
Although the fire was burning brightly, Mrs. Hall was surprised to see that her visitor still wore his hat and coat.
Can I take your hat and coat, sir, and give them a good dry in the kitchen?
I prefer to keep them on.
Very well, sir. As you like.
A guest stopping at Iping in the wintertime was an unheard of piece of luck, let alone a guest who didn't haggle. So Mrs. Hall thanked her luck and ended the conversation.
In a bit, the room will be warmer.
He didn't respond, so Mrs. Hall whisked out of the room.
SLAM
In spite of the guest's cold behavior, Mrs. Hall prepared him a meal with her own hands to show herself worthy of her good fortune.

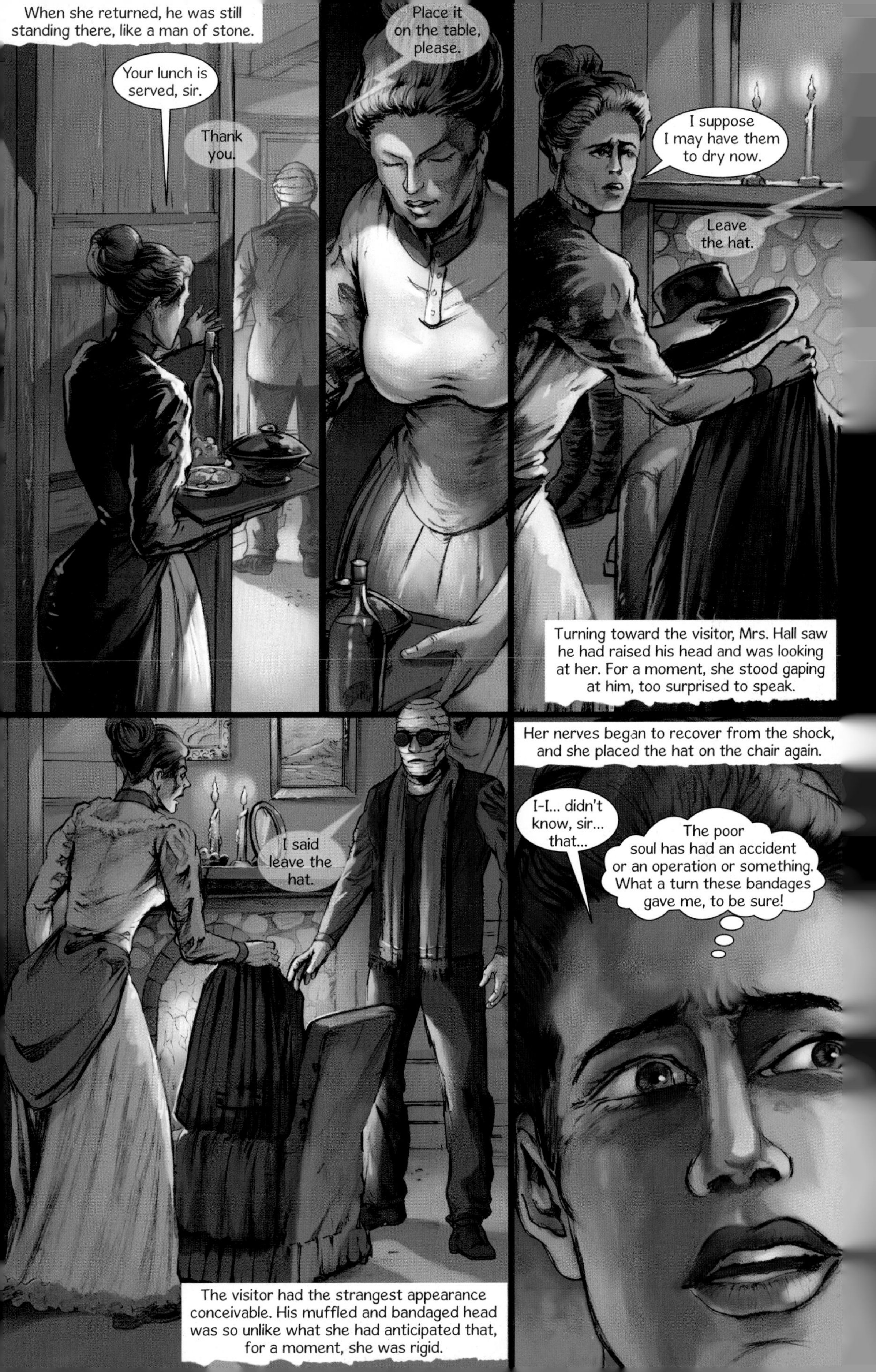
When she returned, he was still standing there, like a man of stone.
Your lunch is served, sir.
Thank you.
Place it on the table, please.
I suppose I may have them to dry now.
Leave the hat.
Turning toward the visitor, Mrs. Hall saw he had raised his head and was looking at her. For a moment, she stood gaping at him, too surprised to speak.
I said leave the hat.
The visitor had the strangest appearance conceivable. His muffled and bandaged head was so unlike what she had anticipated that, for a moment, she was rigid.
Her nerves began to recover from the shock, and she placed the hat on the chair again.
I-I... didn't know, sir... that...
The poor soul has had an accident or an operation or something. What a turn these bandages gave me, to be sure!

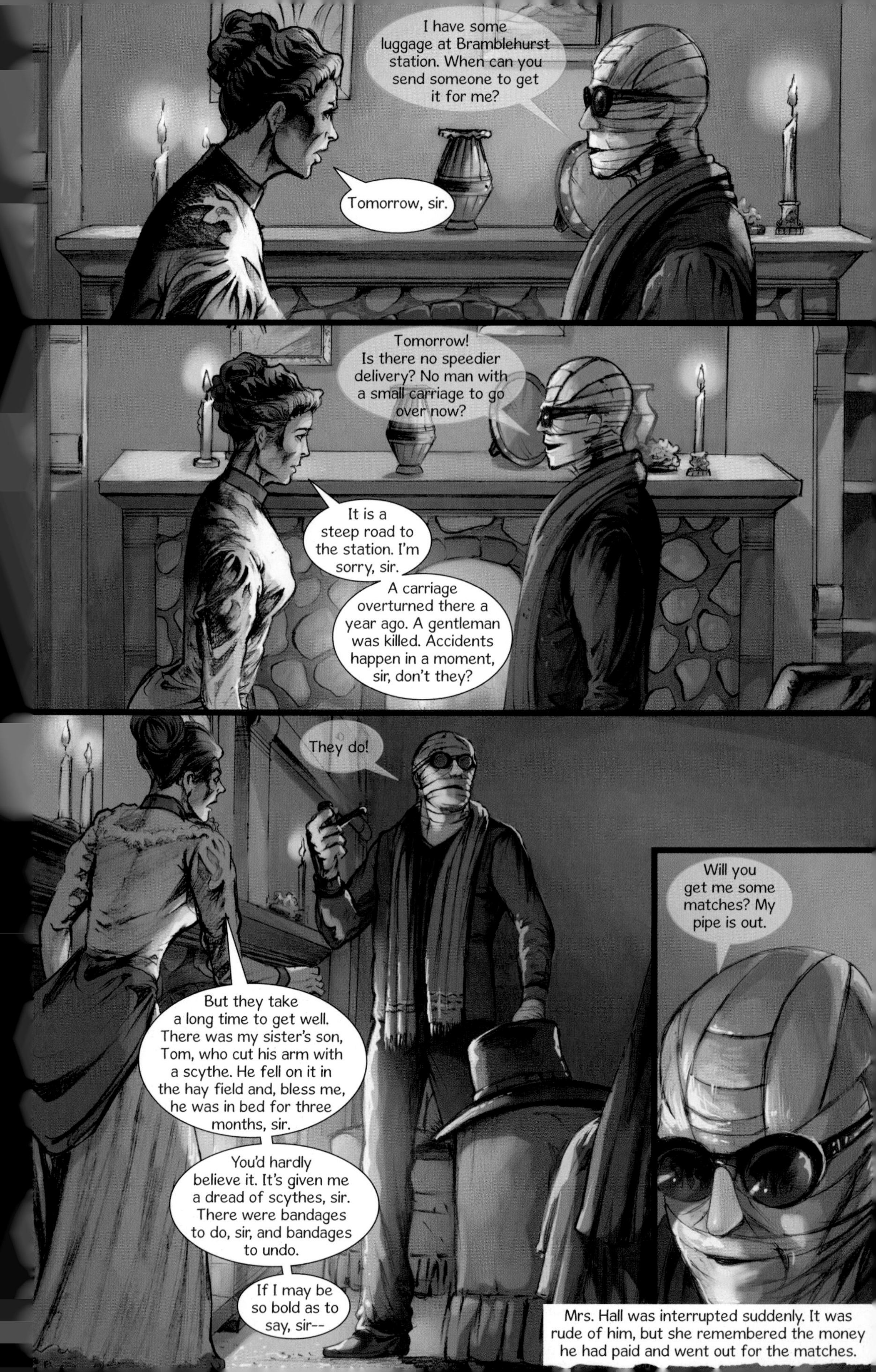

I have some luggage at Bramblehurst station. When can you send someone to get it for me?
Tomorrow, sir.
Tomorrow! Is there no speedier delivery? No man with a small carriage to go over now?
It is a steep road to the station. I'm sorry, sir.
A carriage overturned there a year ago. A gentleman was killed. Accidents happen in a moment, sir, don't they?
They do!
But they take a long time to get well. There was my sister's son, Tom, who cut his arm with a scythe. He fell on it in the hay field and, bless me, he was in bed for three months, sir.
You'd hardly believe it. It's given me a dread of scythes, sir. There were bandages to do, sir, and bandages to undo.
If I may be so bold as to say, sir--
Will you get me some matches? My pipe is out.
Mrs. Hall was interrupted suddenly. It was rude of him, but she remembered the money he had paid and went out for the matches.

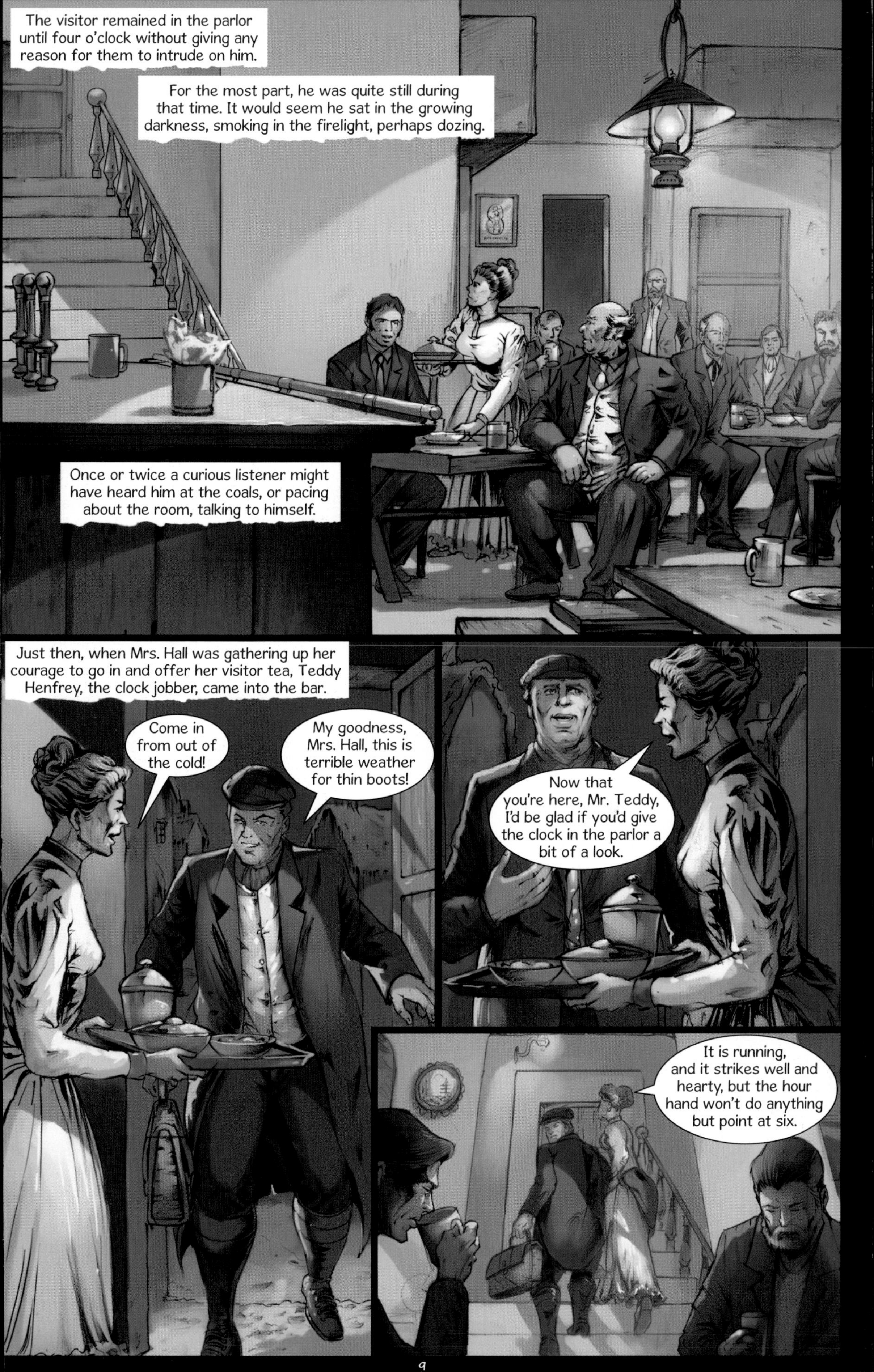

The visitor remained in the parlor until four o'clock without giving any reason for them to intrude on him.
For the most part, he was quite still during that time. It would seem he sat in the growing darkness, smoking in the firelight, perhaps dozing.
Once or twice a curious listener might have heard him at the coals, or pacing about the room, talking to himself.
Just then, when Mrs. Hall was gathering up her courage to go in and offer her visitor tea, Teddy Henfrey, the clock jobber, came into the bar.
Come in from out of the cold!
My goodness, Mrs. Hall, this is terrible weather for thin boots!
Now that you're here, Mr. Teddy, I'd be glad if you'd give the clock in the parlor a bit of a look.
It is running, and it strikes well and hearty, but the hour hand won't do anything but point at six.

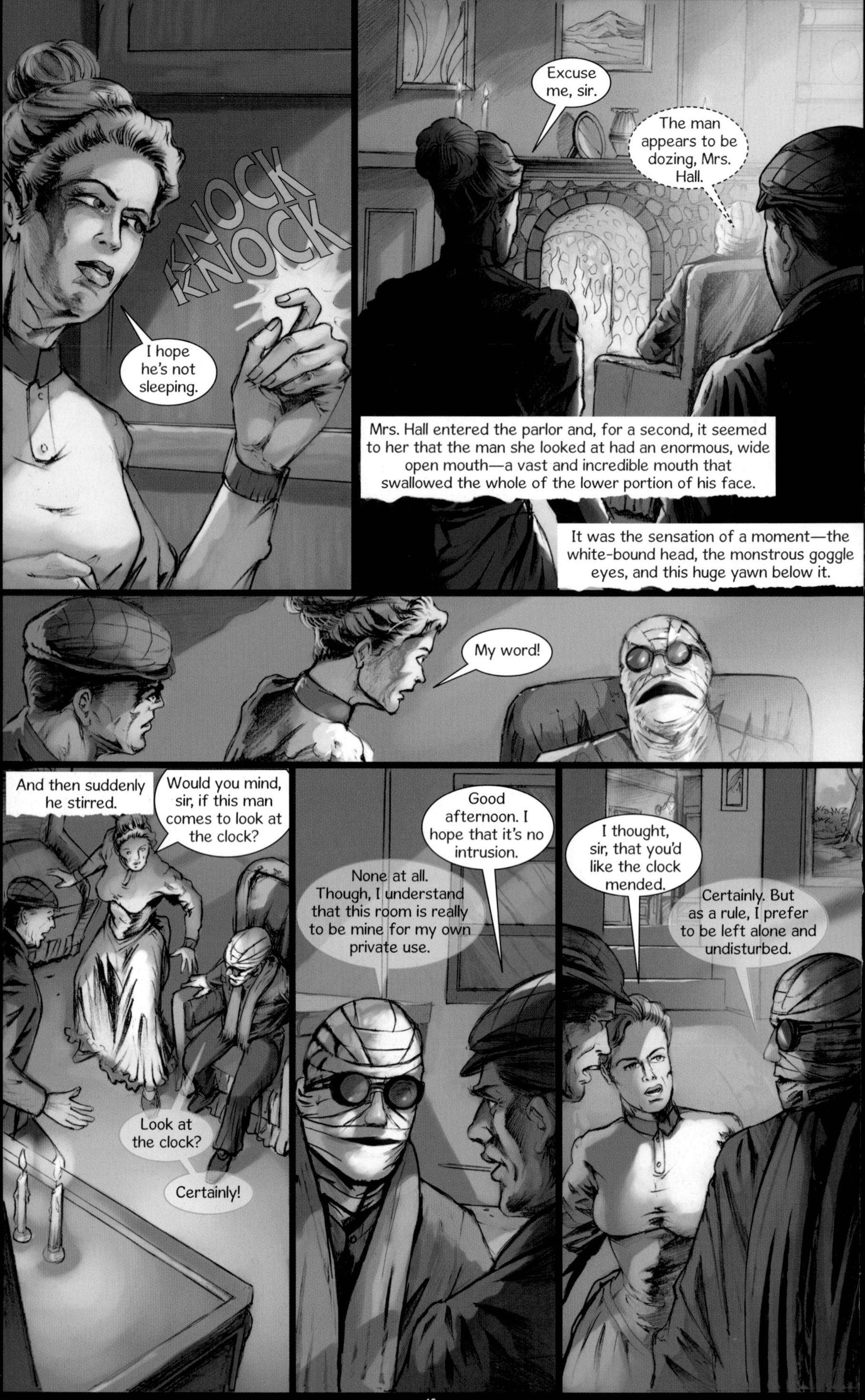

KNOCK KNOCK
I hope he's not sleeping.
Excuse me, sir.
The man appears to be dozing, Mrs. Hall.
Mrs. Hall entered the parlor and, for a second, it seemed to her that the man she looked at had an enormous, wide open mouth—a vast and incredible mouth that swallowed the whole of the lower portion of his face.
It was the sensation of a moment—the white-bound head, the monstrous goggle eyes, and this huge yawn below it.
My word!
And then suddenly he stirred.
Would you mind, sir, if this man comes to look at the clock?
Look at the clock?
Certainly!
Good afternoon. I hope that it's no intrusion.
None at all. Though, I understand that this room is really to be mine for my own private use.
I thought, sir, that you'd like the clock mended.
Certainly. But as a rule, I prefer to be left alone and undisturbed.

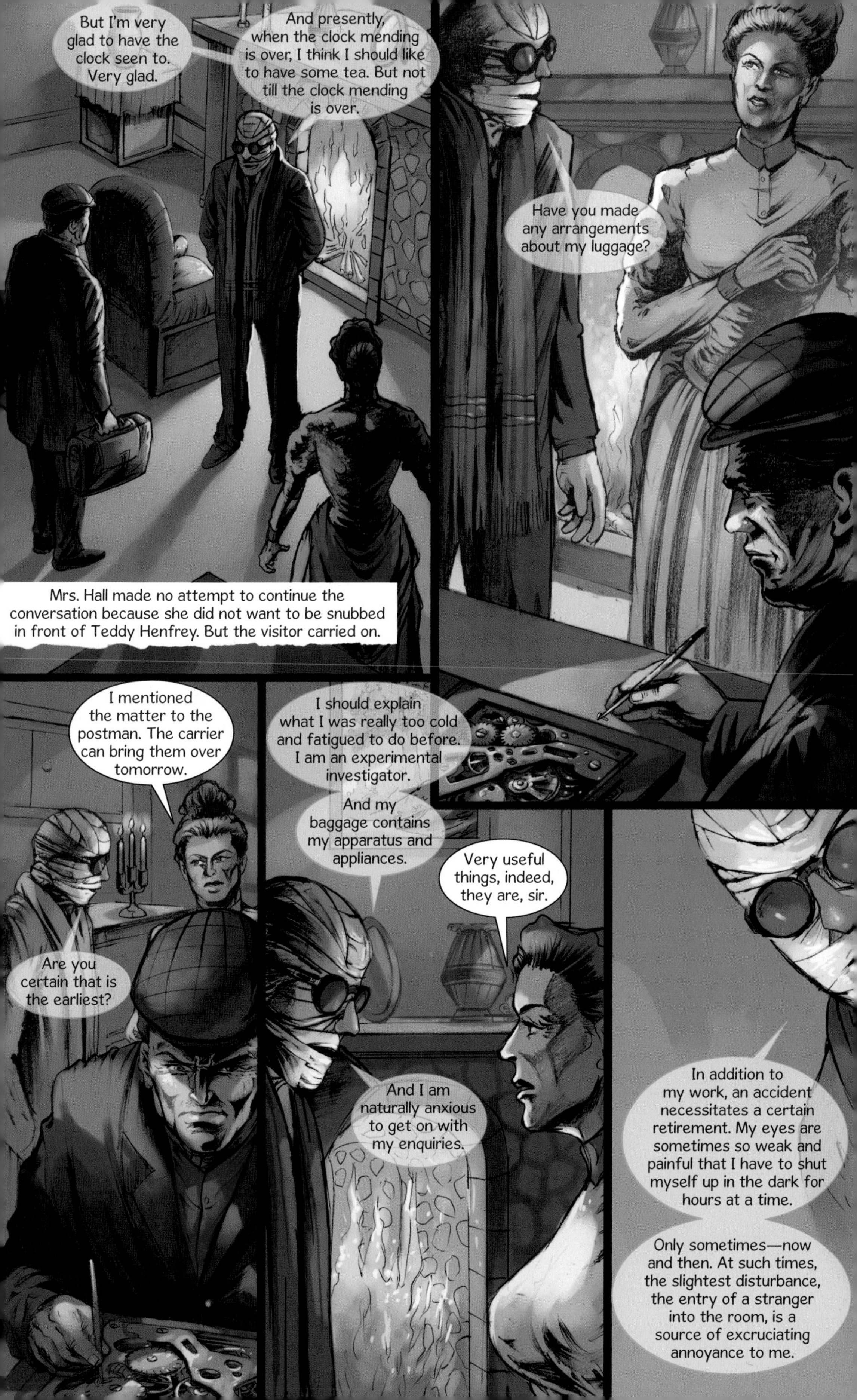
But I'm very glad to have the clock seen to. Very glad.
And presently, when the clock mending is over, I think I should like to have some tea. But not till the clock mending is over.
Mrs. Hall made no attempt to continue the conversation because she did not want to be snubbed in front of Teddy Henfrey. But the visitor carried on.
Have you made any arrangements about my luggage?
I mentioned the matter to the postman. The carrier can bring them over tomorrow.
Are you certain that is the earliest?
I should explain what I was really too cold and fatigued to do before. I am an experimental investigator.
And my baggage contains my apparatus and appliances.
Very useful things, indeed, they are, sir.
And I am naturally anxious to get on with my enquiries.
In addition to my work, an accident necessitates a certain retirement. My eyes are sometimes so weak and painful that I have to shut myself up in the dark for hours at a time.
Only sometimes—now and then. At such times, the slightest disturbance, the entry of a stranger into the room, is a source of excruciating annoyance to me.

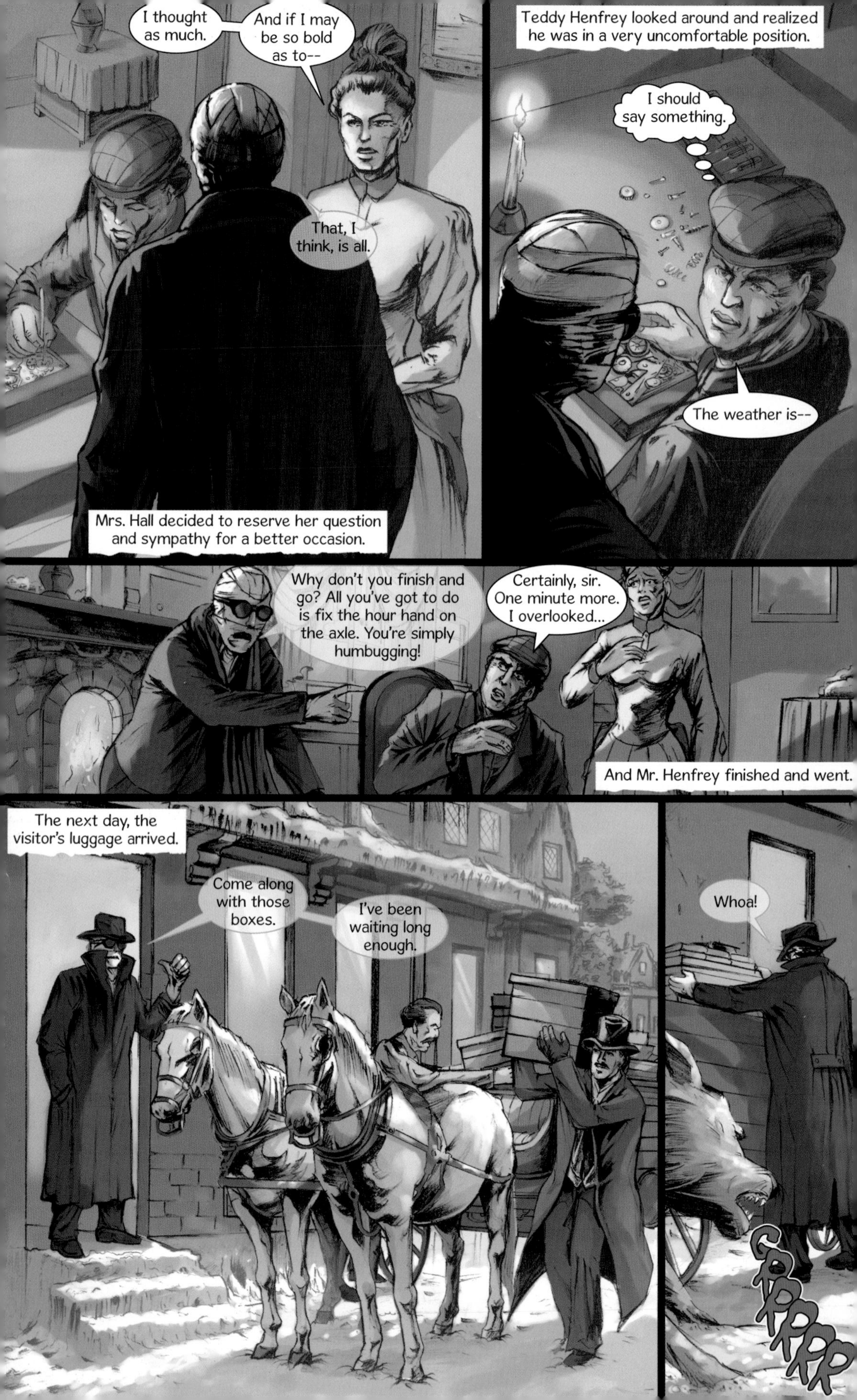
I thought as much.
And if I may be so bold as to--
That, I think, is all.
Mrs. Hall decided to reserve her question and sympathy for a better occasion.
Teddy Henfrey looked around and realized he was in a very uncomfortable position.
I should say something.
The weather is--
Why don't you finish and go? All you've got to do is fix the hour hand on the axle. You're simply humbugging!
Certainly, sir. One minute more. I overlooked...
And Mr. Henfrey finished and went.
The next day, the visitor's luggage arrived.
Come along with those boxes.
I've been waiting long enough.
Whoa!
GRRRRR

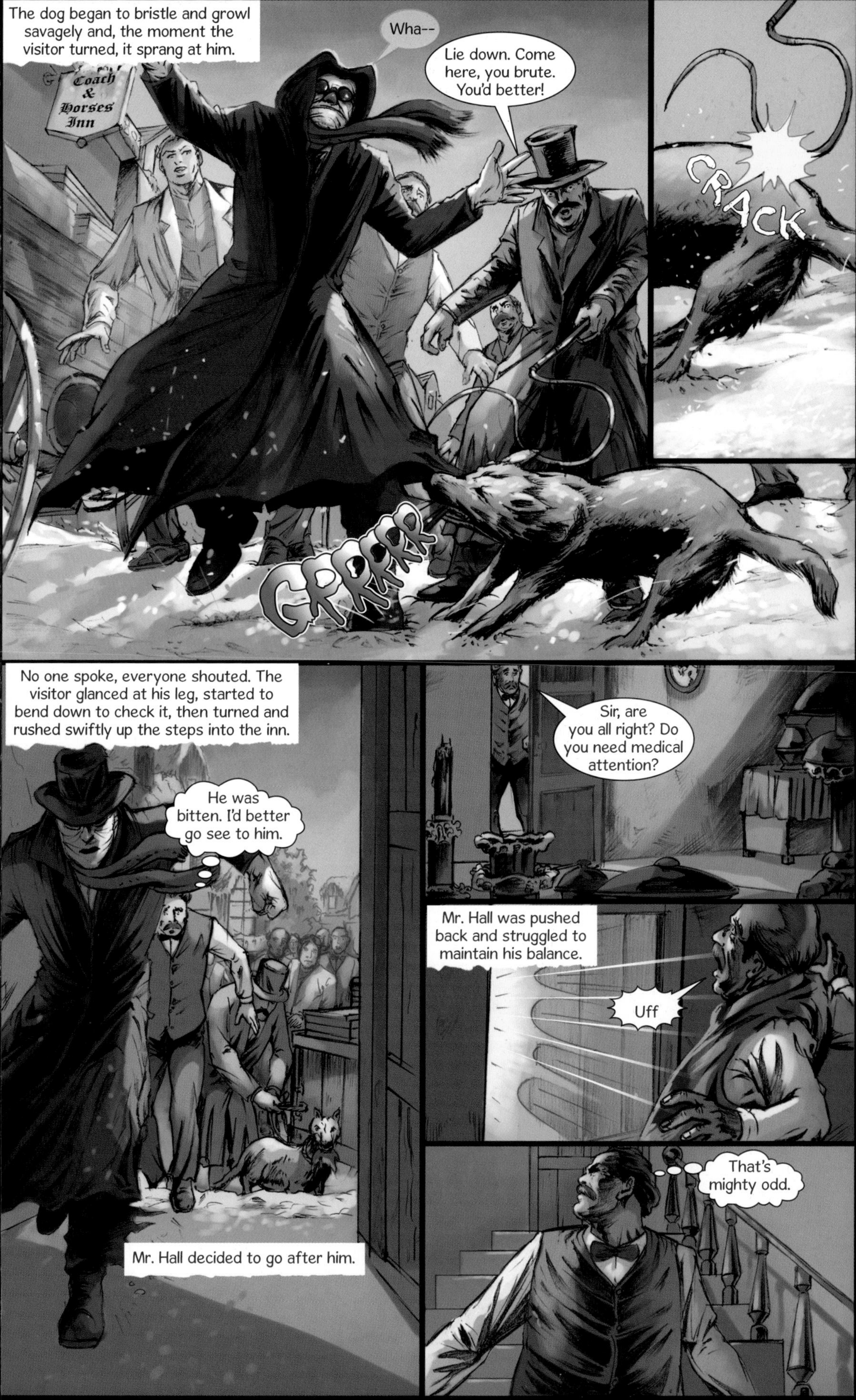

The dog began to bristle and growl savagely and, the moment the visitor turned, it sprang at him.
Wha--
Lie down. Come here, you brute. You'd better!
Coach & Horses Inn
CRACK
GRRRRR
No one spoke, everyone shouted. The visitor glanced at his leg, started to bend down to check it, then turned and rushed swiftly up the steps into the inn.
He was bitten. I'd better go see to him.
Mr. Hall decided to go after him.
Sir, are you all right? Do you need medical attention?
Mr. Hall was pushed back and struggled to maintain his balance.
Uff
That's mighty odd.

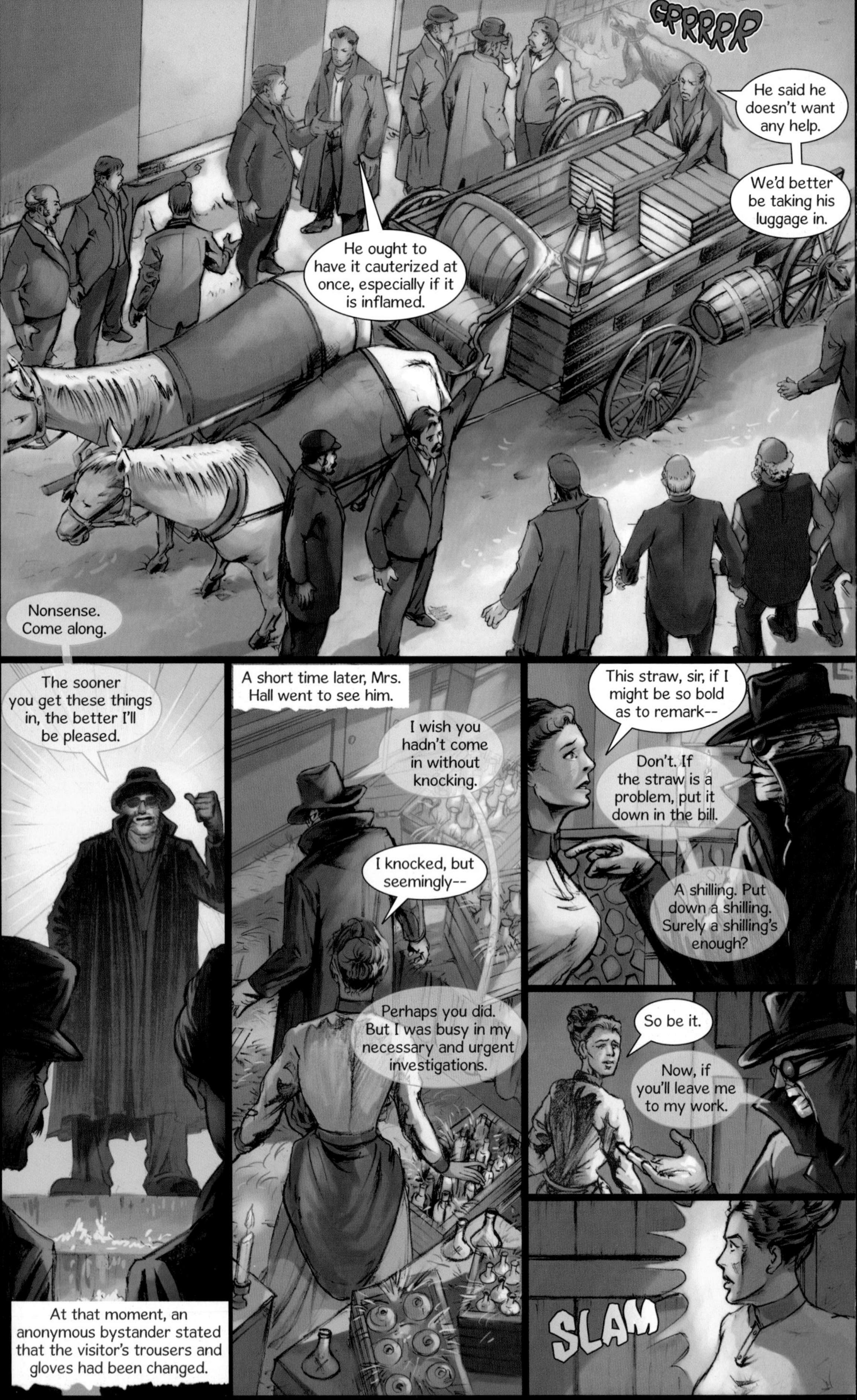
GRRRRR
He said he doesn't want any help.
We'd better be taking his luggage in.
He ought to have it cauterized at once, especially if it is inflamed.
Nonsense. Come along.
The sooner you get these things in, the better I'll be pleased.
At that moment, an anonymous bystander stated that the visitor's trousers and gloves had been changed.
A short time later, Mrs. Hall went to see him.
I wish you hadn't come in without knocking.
I knocked, but seemingly--
Perhaps you did. But I was busy in my necessary and urgent investigations.
This straw, sir, if I might be so bold as to remark--
Don't. If the straw is a problem, put it down in the bill.
A shilling. Put down a shilling. Surely a shilling's enough?
So be it.
Now, if you'll leave me to my work.
SLAM

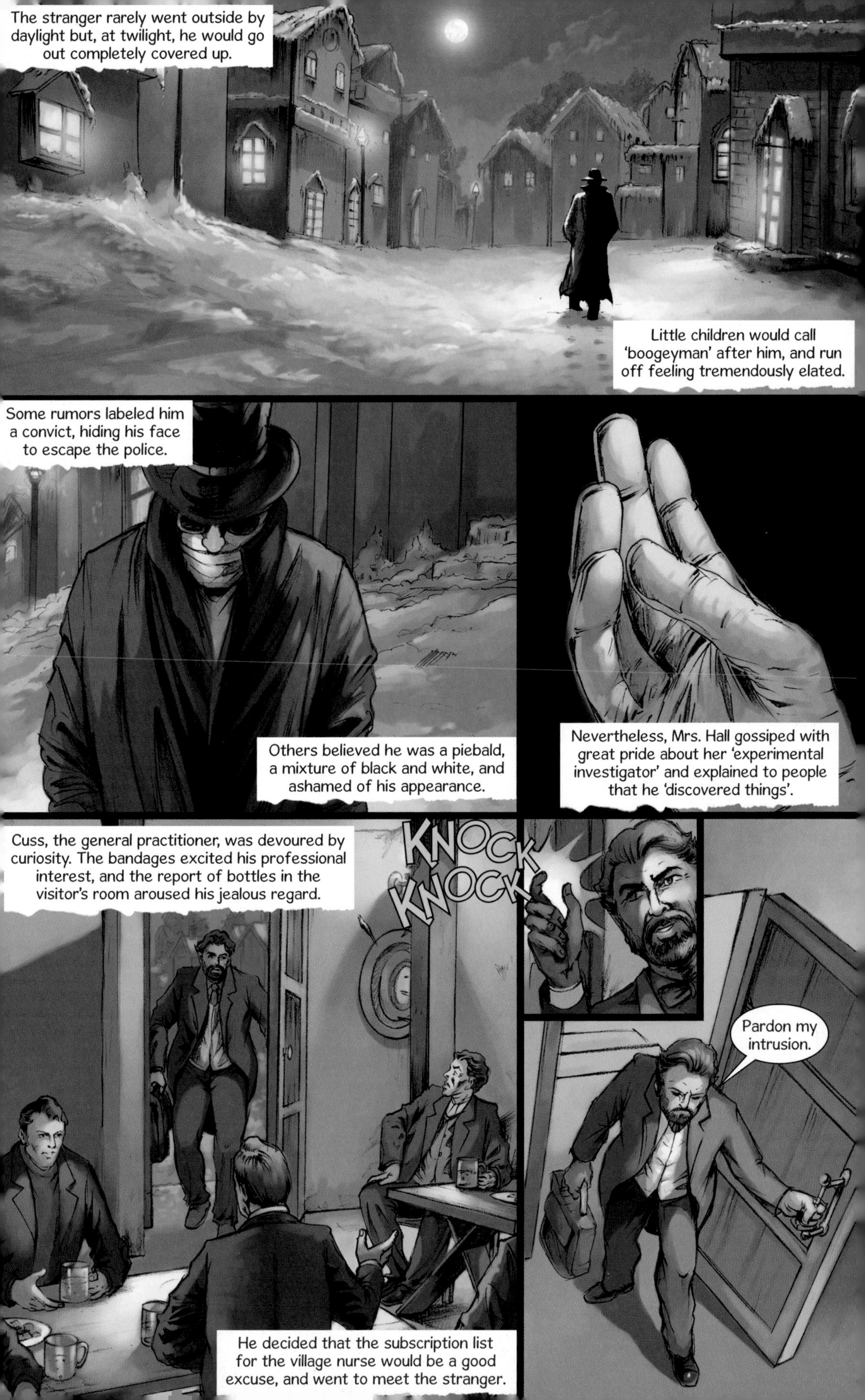
The stranger rarely went outside by daylight but, at twilight, he would go out completely covered up.
Little children would call 'boogeyman' after him, and run off feeling tremendously elated.
Some rumors labeled him a convict, hiding his face to escape the police.
Others believed he was a piebald, a mixture of black and white, and ashamed of his appearance.
Nevertheless, Mrs. Hall gossiped with great pride about her 'experimental investigator' and explained to people that he 'discovered things'.
Cuss, the general practitioner, was devoured by curiosity. The bandages excited his professional interest, and the report of bottles in the visitor's room aroused his jealous regard.
KNOCK KNOCK
He decided that the subscription list for the village nurse would be a good excuse, and went to meet the stranger.
Pardon my intrusion.

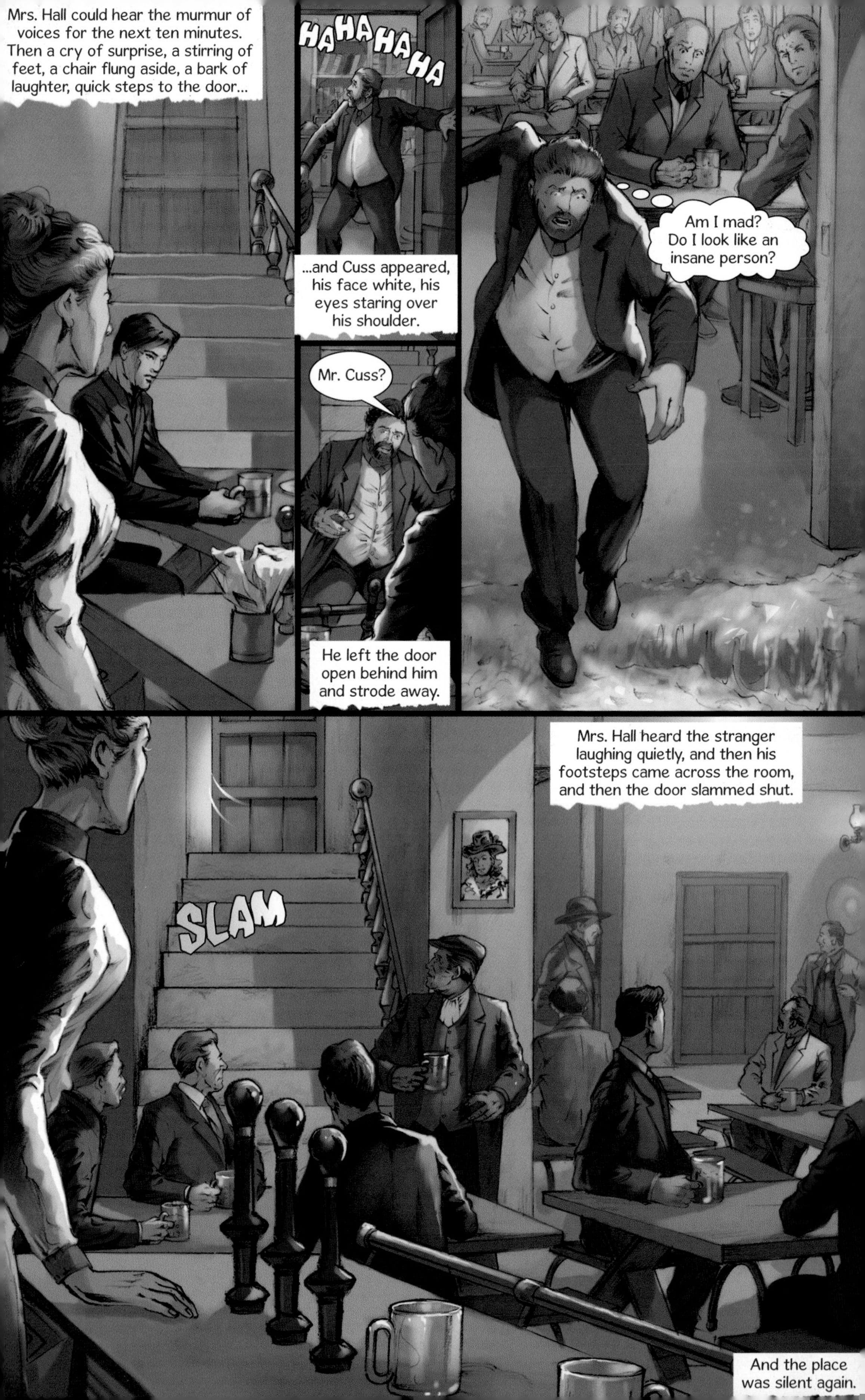
Mrs. Hall could hear the murmur of voices for the next ten minutes. Then a cry of surprise, a stirring of feet, a chair flung aside, a bark of laughter, quick steps to the door...
HAHAHAHA
...and Cuss appeared, his face white, his eyes staring over his shoulder.
Mr. Cuss?
He left the door open behind him and strode away.
Am I mad? Do I look like an insane person?
Mrs. Hall heard the stranger laughing quietly, and then his footsteps came across the room, and then the door slammed shut.
SLAM
And the place was silent again.

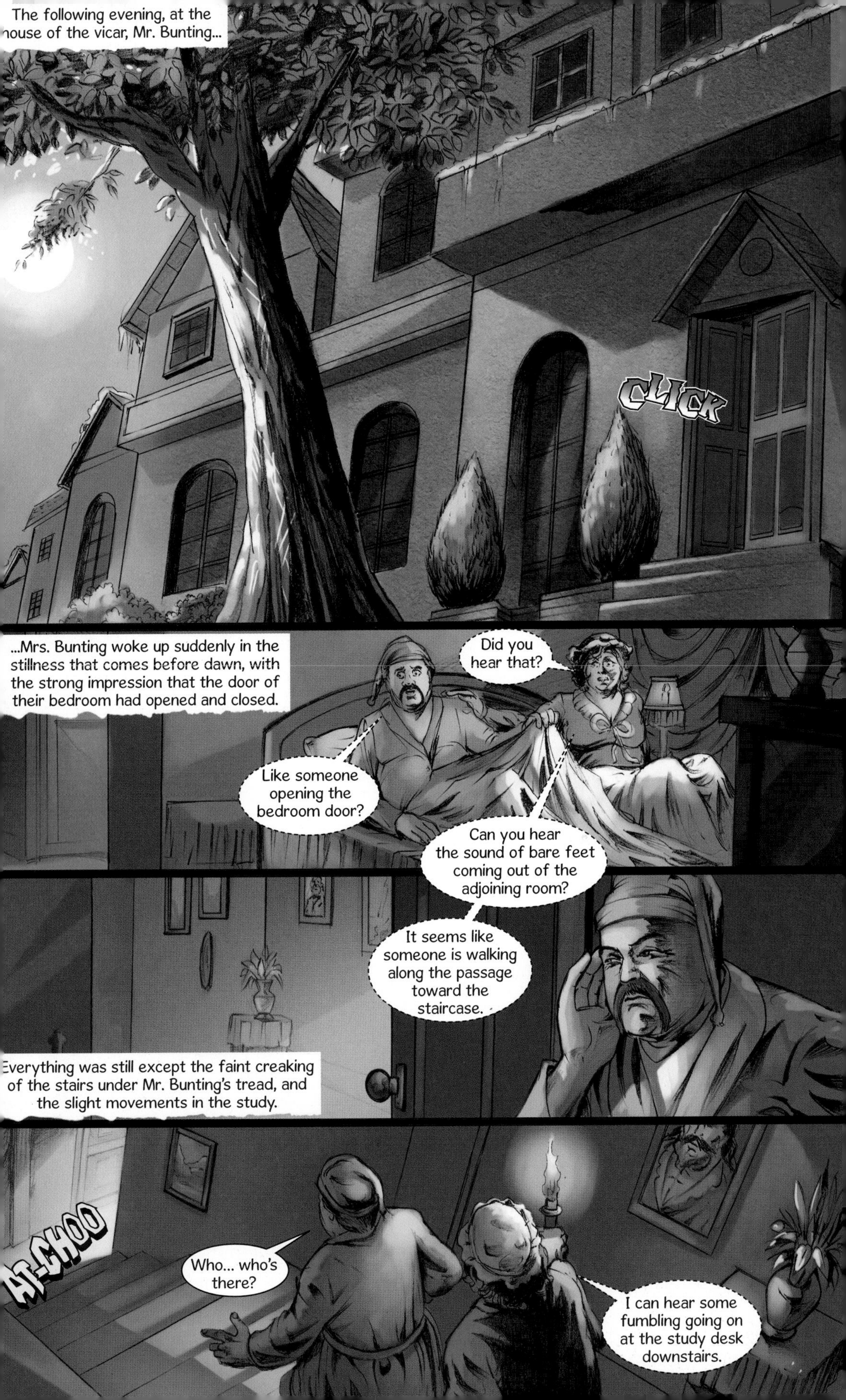
The following evening, at the house of the vicar, Mr. Bunting...
CLICK
...Mrs. Bunting woke up suddenly in the stillness that comes before dawn, with the strong impression that the door of their bedroom had opened and closed.
Did you hear that?
Like someone opening the bedroom door?
Can you hear the sound of bare feet coming out of the adjoining room?
It seems like someone is walking along the passage toward the staircase.
Everything was still except the faint creaking of the stairs under Mr. Bunting's tread, and the slight movements in the study.
AT-CHOO
Who... who's there?
I can hear some fumbling going on at the study desk downstairs.

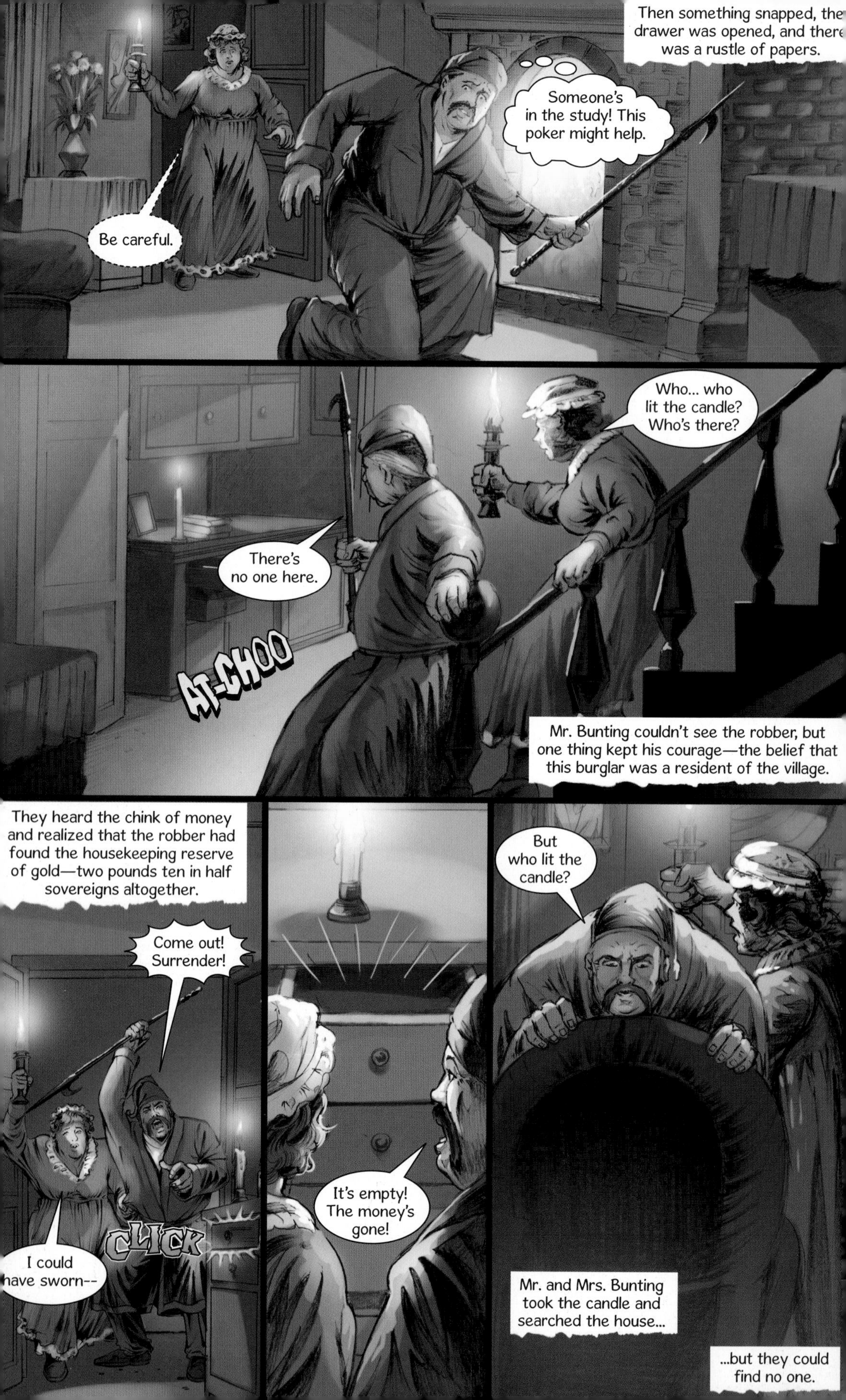

Then something snapped, the drawer was opened, and there was a rustle of papers.
Be careful.
Someone's in the study! This poker might help.
Who... who lit the candle? Who's there?
There's no one here.
AT-CHOO
Mr. Bunting couldn't see the robber, but one thing kept his courage—the belief that this burglar was a resident of the village.
They heard the chink of money and realized that the robber had found the housekeeping reserve of gold—two pounds ten in half sovereigns altogether.
Come out! Surrender!
I could have sworn--
CLICK
It's empty! The money's gone!
But who lit the candle?
Mr. and Mrs. Bunting took the candle and searched the house...
...but they could find no one.

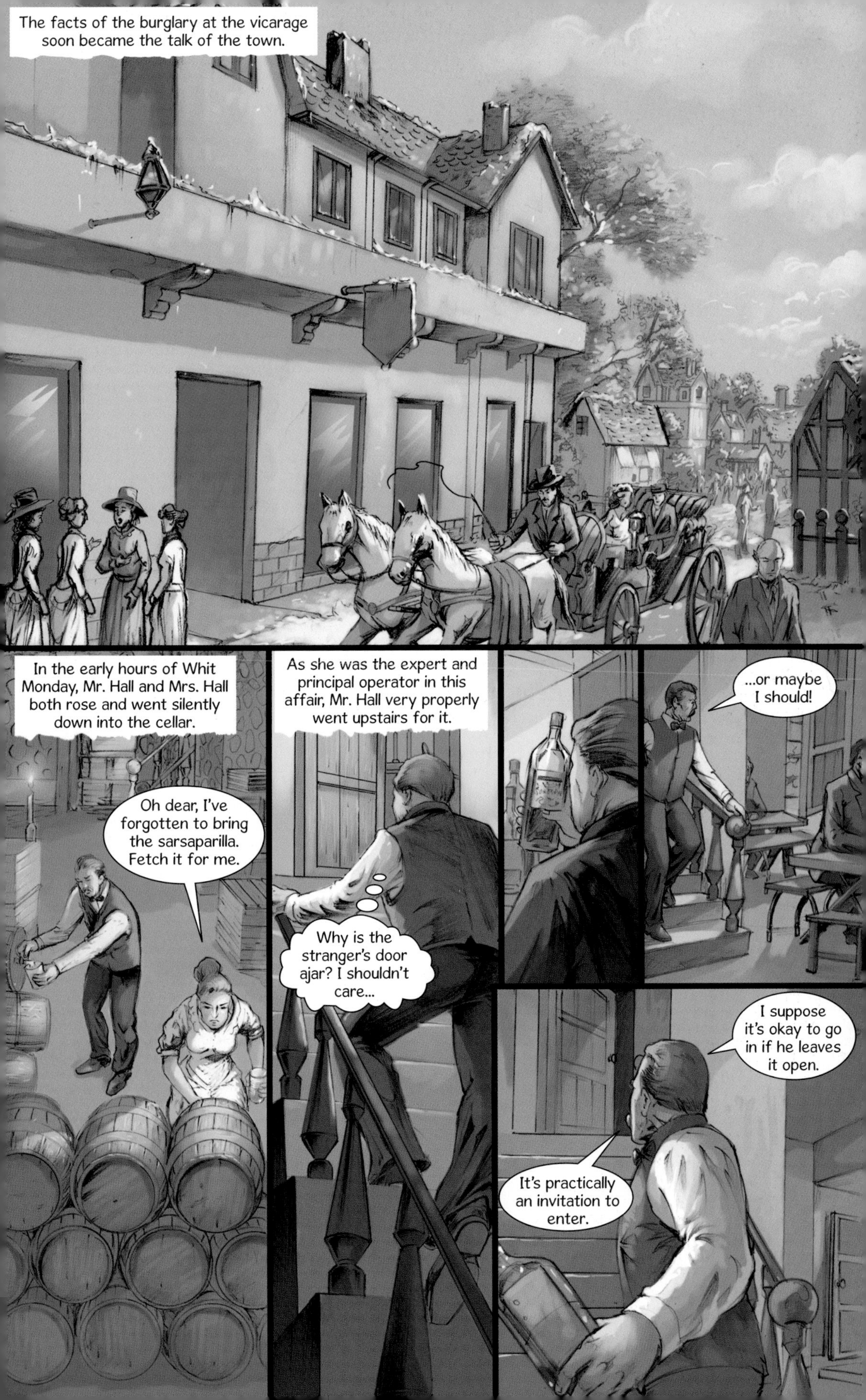
The facts of the burglary at the vicarage soon became the talk of the town.
In the early hours of Whit Monday, Mr. Hall and Mrs. Hall both rose and went silently down into the cellar.
Oh dear, I've forgotten to bring the sarsaparilla. Fetch it for me.
As she was the expert and principal operator in this affair, Mr. Hall very properly went upstairs for it.
Why is the stranger's door ajar? I shouldn't care...
...or maybe I should!
I suppose it's okay to go in if he leaves it open.
It's practically an invitation to enter.

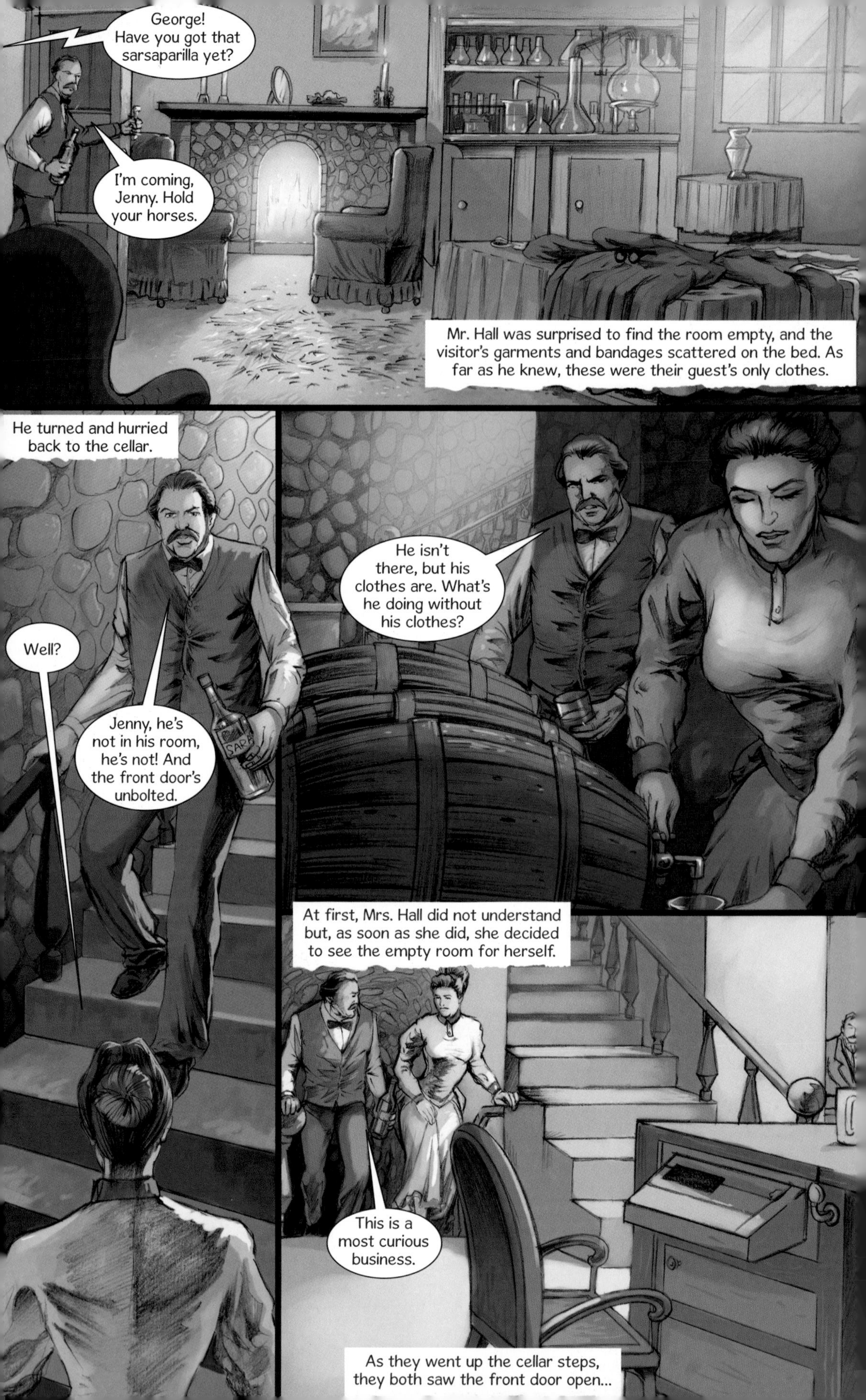
George! Have you got that sarsaparilla yet?
I'm coming, Jenny. Hold your horses.
Mr. Hall was surprised to find the room empty, and the visitor's garments and bandages scattered on the bed. As far as he knew, these were their guest's only clothes.
He turned and hurried back to the cellar.
Well?
Jenny, he's not in his room, he's not! And the front door's unbolted.
SARA
He isn't there, but his clothes are. What's he doing without his clothes?
At first, Mrs. Hall did not understand but, as soon as she did, she decided to see the empty room for herself.
This is a most curious business.
As they went up the cellar steps, they both saw the front door open...

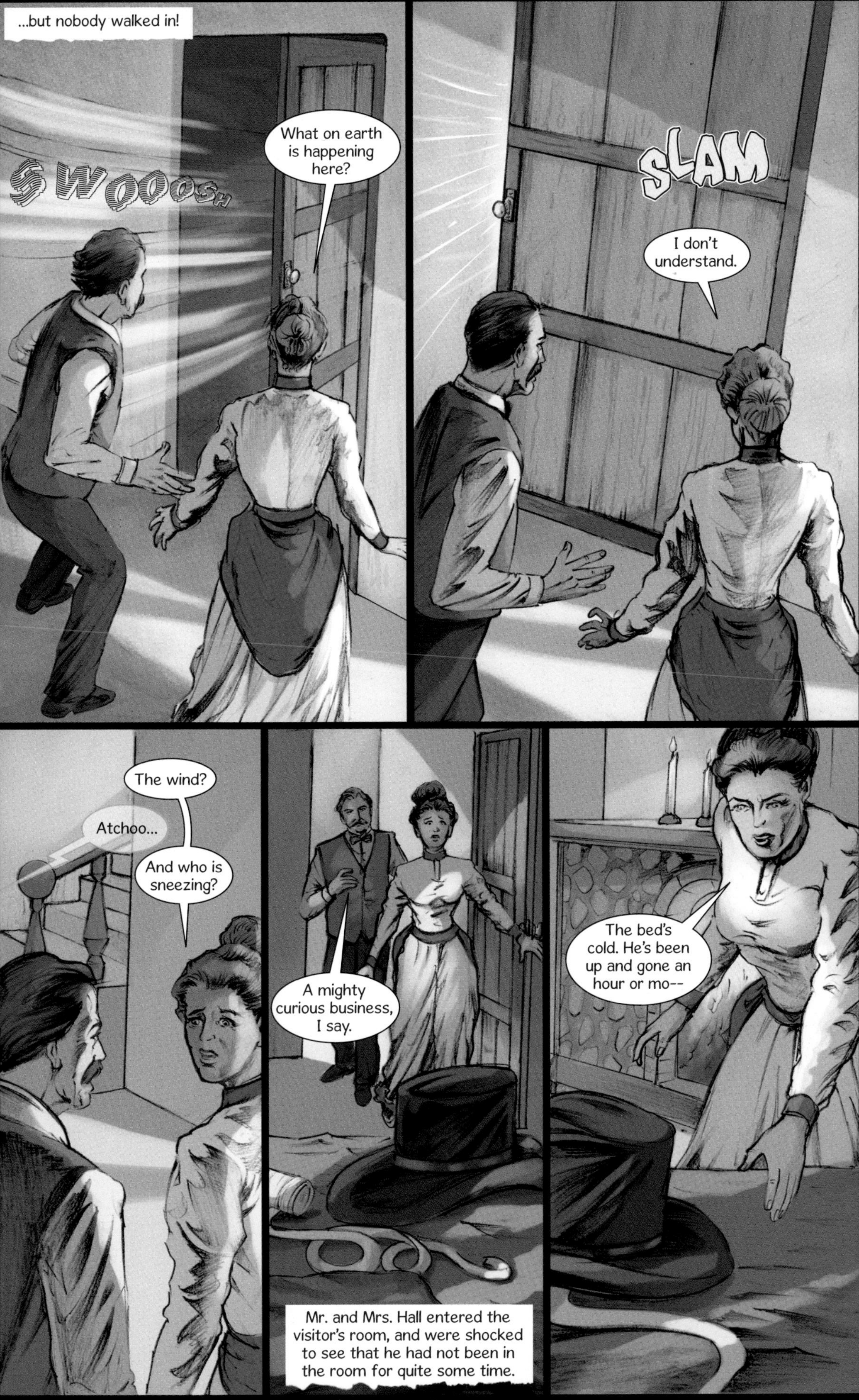
...but nobody walked in!
SWOOOSH
What on earth is happening here?
SLAM
I don't understand.
The wind?
Atchoo...
And who is sneezing?
A mighty curious business, I say.
Mr. and Mrs. Hall entered the visitor's room, and were shocked to see that he had not been in the room for quite some time.
The bed's cold. He's been up and gone an hour or mo--

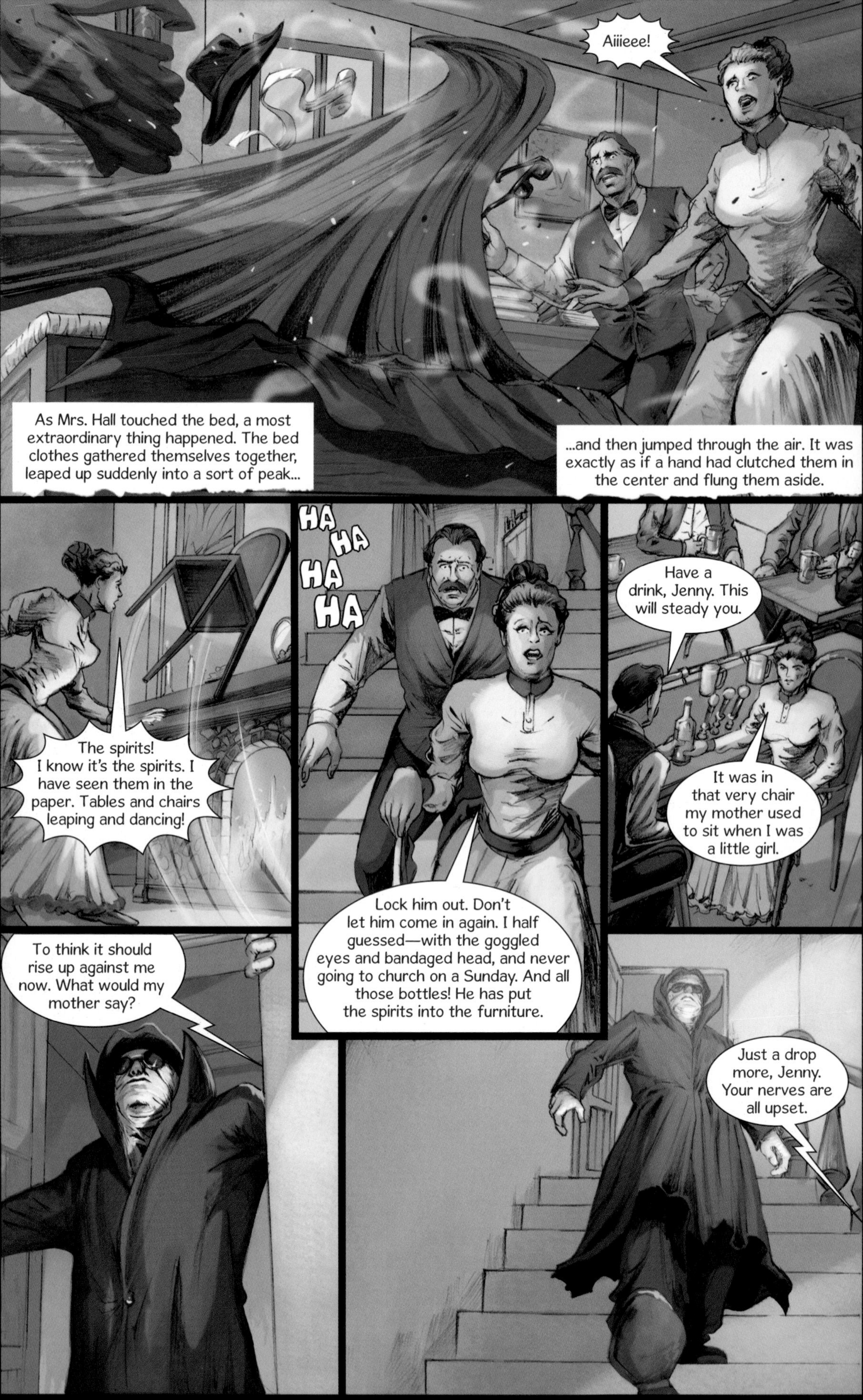
Aiiieee!
As Mrs. Hall touched the bed, a most extraordinary thing happened. The bed clothes gathered themselves together, leaped up suddenly into a sort of peak...
...and then jumped through the air. It was exactly as if a hand had clutched them in the center and flung them aside.
The spirits! I know it's the spirits. I have seen them in the paper. Tables and chairs leaping and dancing!
HA HA HA HA
Lock him out. Don't let him come in again. I half guessed—with the goggled eyes and bandaged head, and never going to church on a Sunday. And all those bottles! He has put the spirits into the furniture.
Have a drink, Jenny. This will steady you.
It was in that very chair my mother used to sit when I was a little girl.
To think it should rise up against me now. What would my mother say?
Just a drop more, Jenny. Your nerves are all upset.

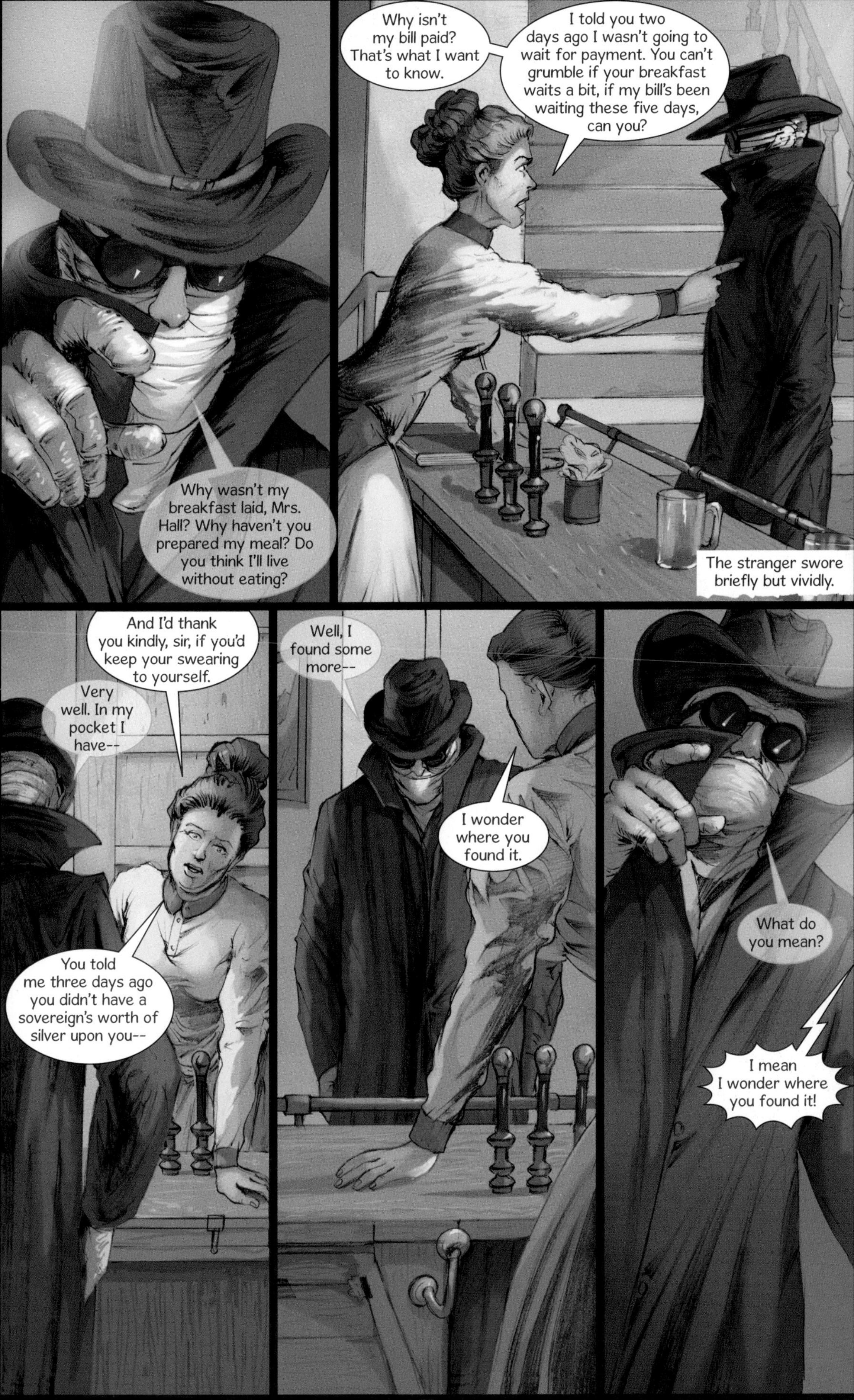
Why wasn't my breakfast laid, Mrs. Hall? Why haven't you prepared my meal? Do you think I'll live without eating?
Why isn't my bill paid? That's what I want to know.
I told you two days ago I wasn't going to wait for payment. You can't grumble if your breakfast waits a bit, if my bill's been waiting these five days, can you?
The stranger swore briefly but vividly.
And I'd thank you kindly, sir, if you'd keep your swearing to yourself.
Very well. In my pocket I have--
You told me three days ago you didn't have a sovereign's worth of silver upon you--
Well, I found some more--
I wonder where you found it.
What do you mean?
I mean I wonder where you found it!

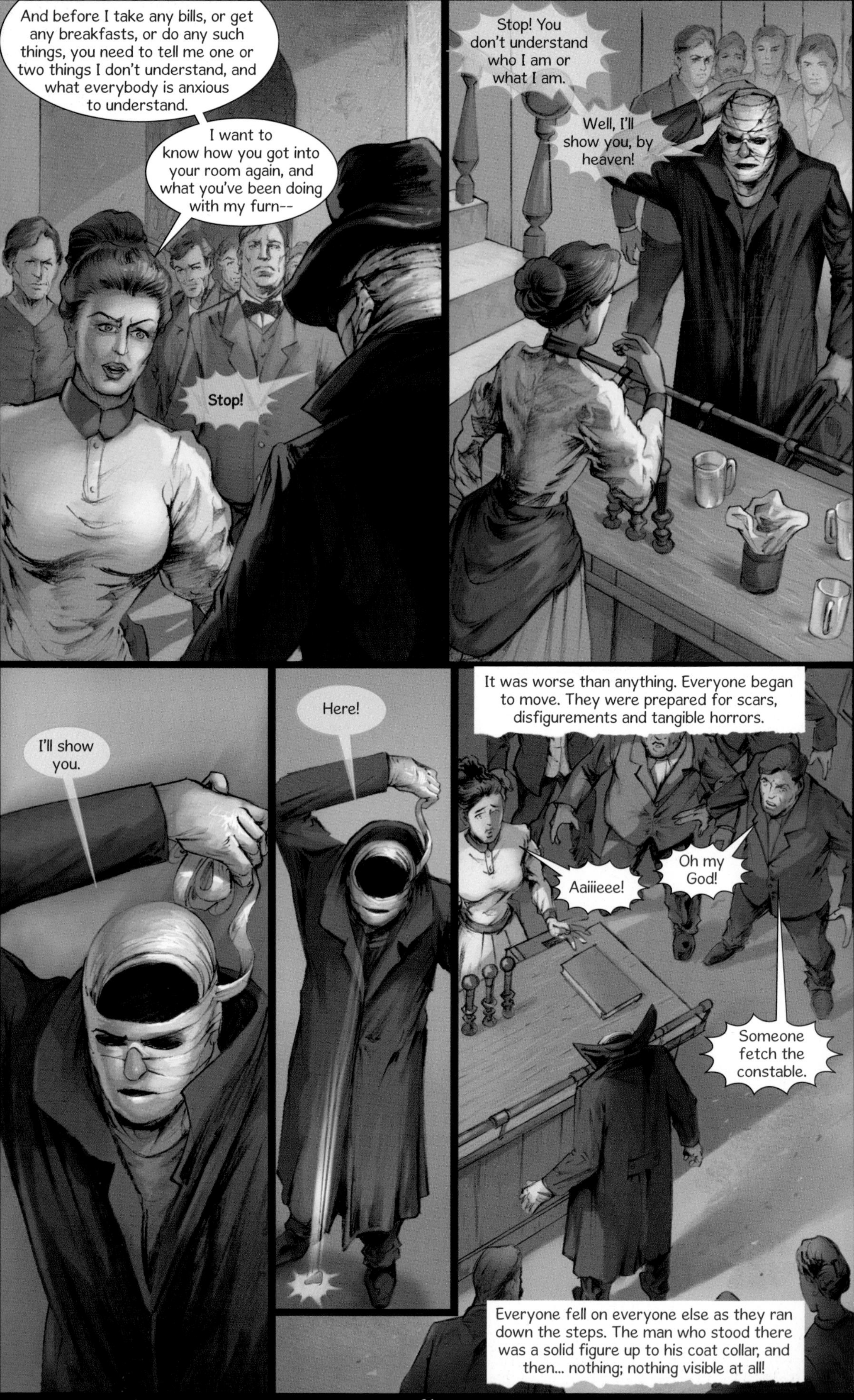
And before I take any bills, or get any breakfasts, or do any such things, you need to tell me one or two things I don't understand, and what everybody is anxious to understand.
I want to know how you got into your room again, and what you've been doing with my furn--
Stop!
Stop! You don't understand who I am or what I am.
Well, I'll show you, by heaven!
I'll show you.
Here!
It was worse than anything. Everyone began to move. They were prepared for scars, disfigurements and tangible horrors.
Aaiiieee!
Oh my God!
Someone fetch the constable.
Everyone fell on everyone else as they ran down the steps. The man who stood there was a solid figure up to his coat collar, and then... nothing; nothing visible at all!

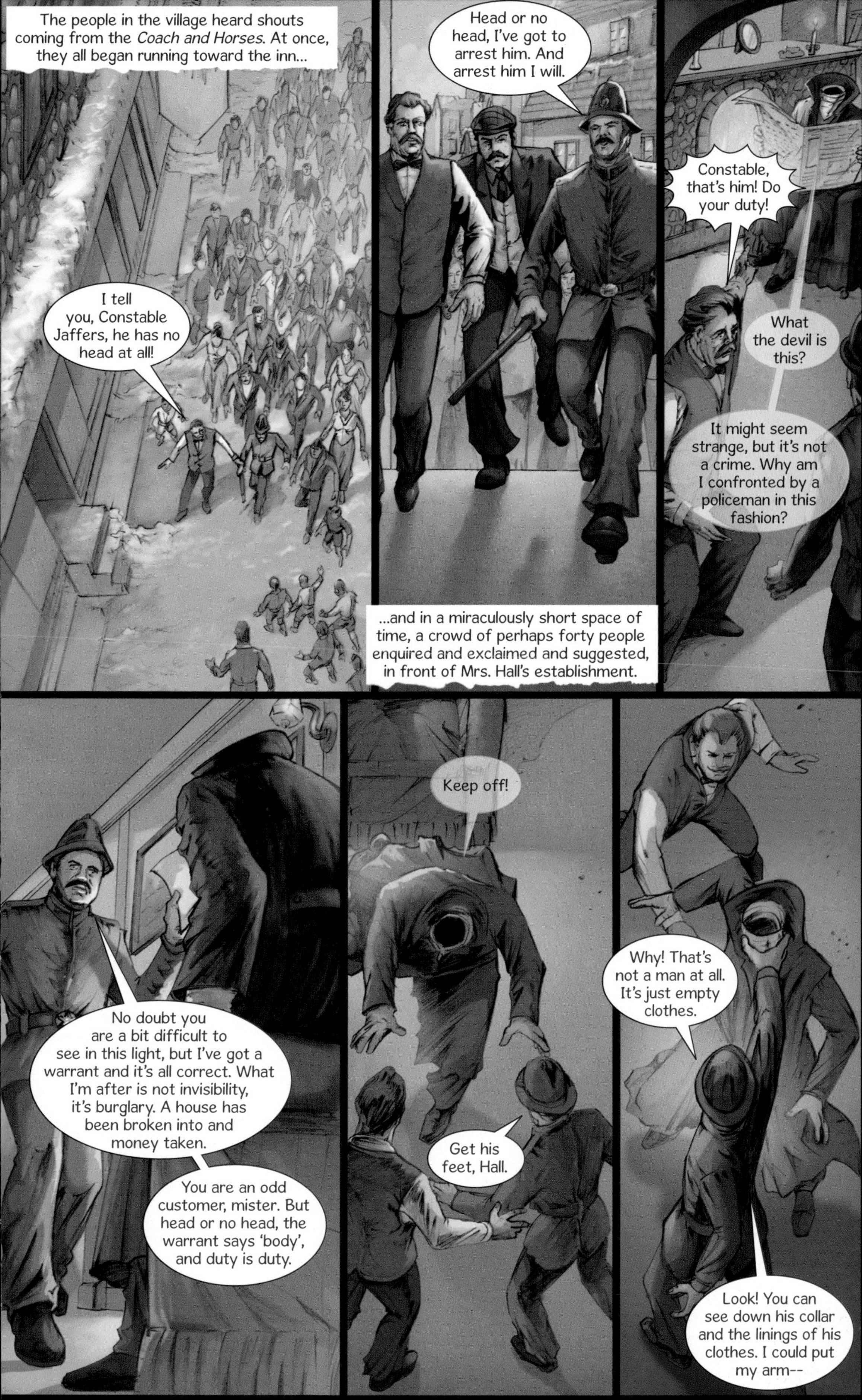
The people in the village heard shouts coming from the *Coach and Horses*. At once, they all began running toward the inn...
I tell you, Constable Jaffers, he has no head at all!
Head or no head, I've got to arrest him. And arrest him I will.
...and in a miraculously short space of time, a crowd of perhaps forty people enquired and exclaimed and suggested, in front of Mrs. Hall's establishment.
Constable, that's him! Do your duty!
What the devil is this?
It might seem strange, but it's not a crime. Why am I confronted by a policeman in this fashion?
No doubt you are a bit difficult to see in this light, but I've got a warrant and it's all correct. What I'm after is not invisibility, it's burglary. A house has been broken into and money taken.
You are an odd customer, mister. But head or no head, the warrant says 'body', and duty is duty.
Keep off!
Get his feet, Hall.
Why! That's not a man at all. It's just empty clothes.
Look! You can see down his collar and the linings of his clothes. I could put my arm--

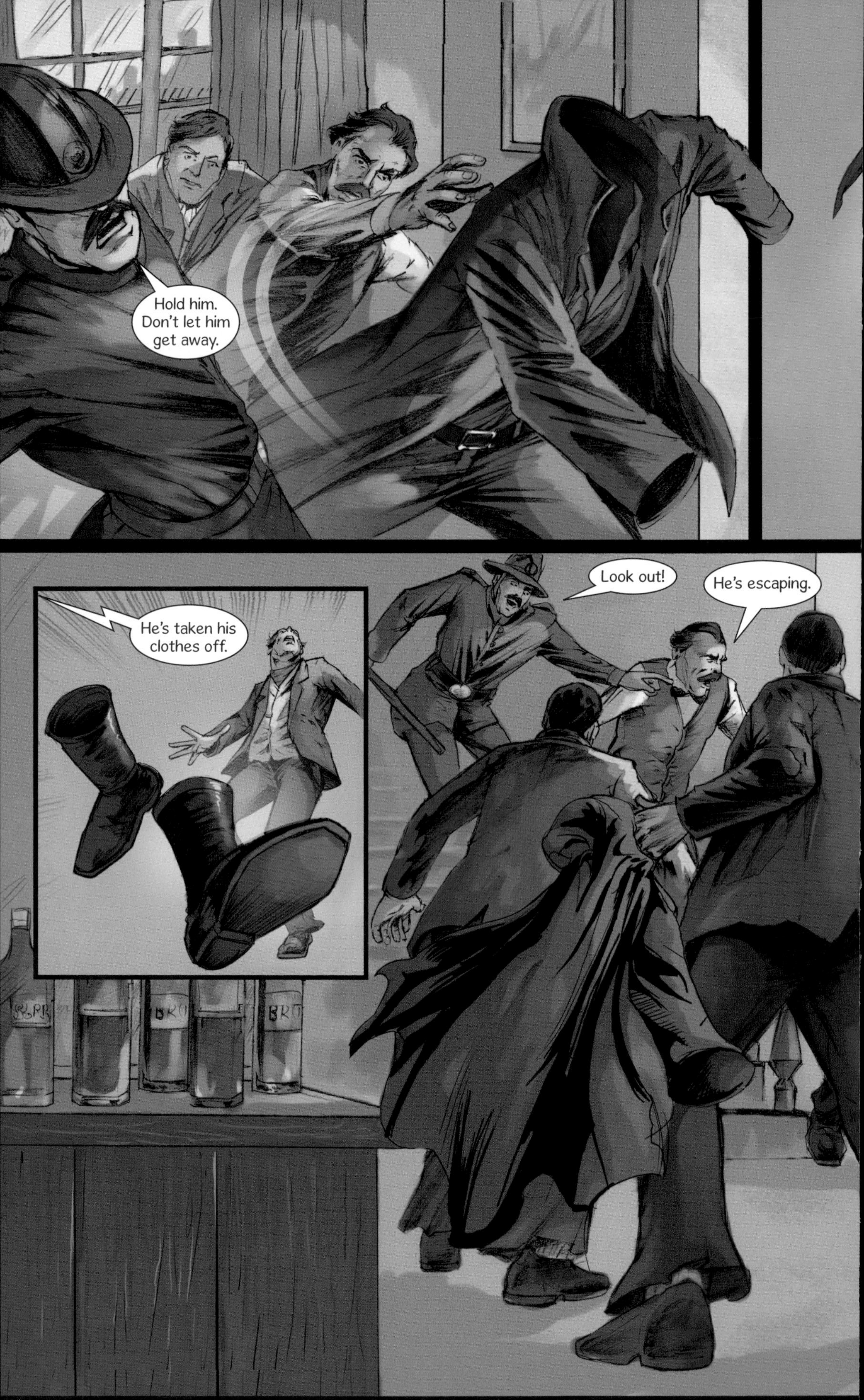
Hold him. Don't let him get away.
He's taken his clothes off.
Look out!
He's escaping.

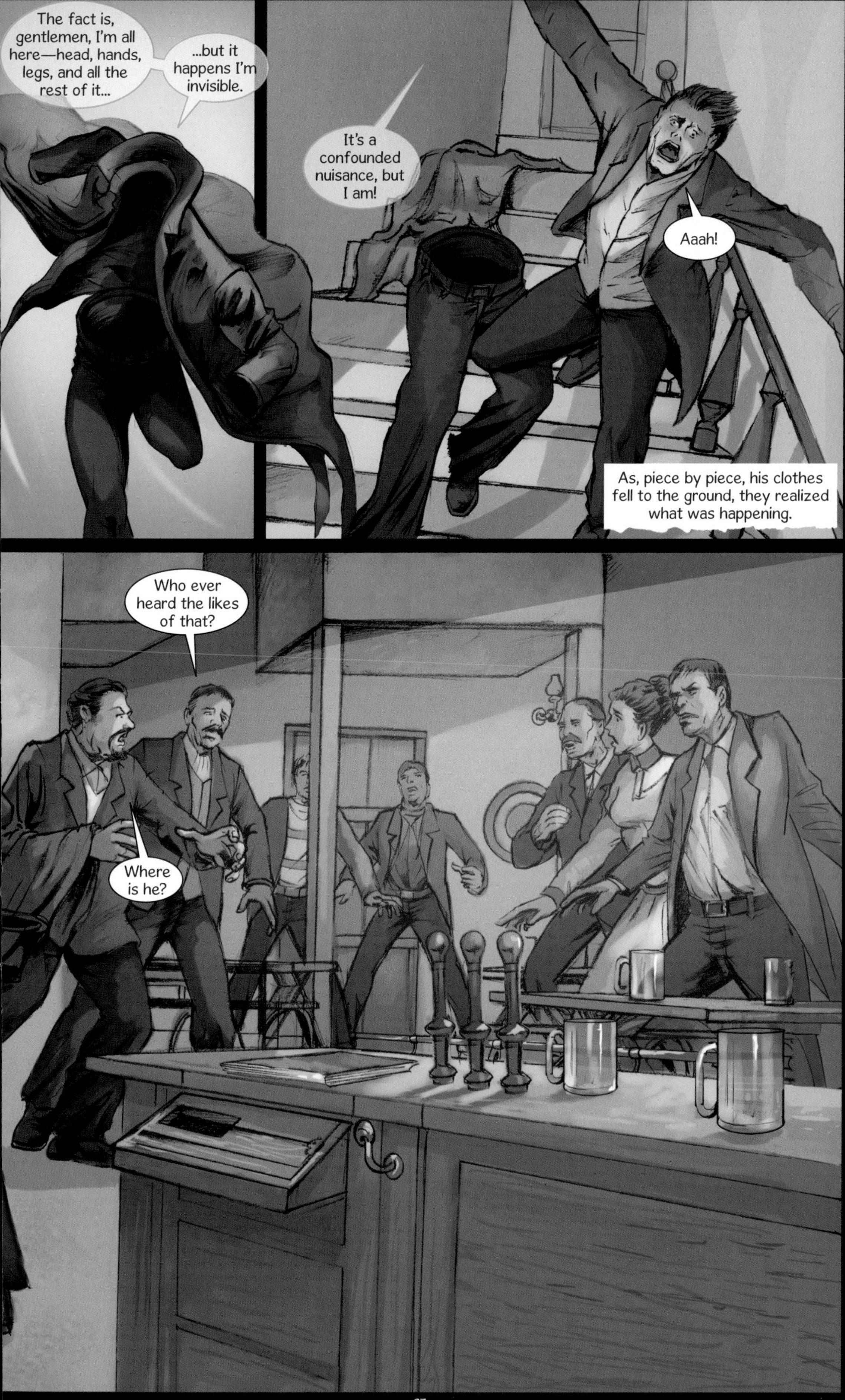
The fact is, gentlemen, I'm all here—head, hands, legs, and all the rest of it...
...but it happens I'm invisible.
It's a confounded nuisance, but I am!
Aaah!
As, piece by piece, his clothes fell to the ground, they realized what was happening.
Who ever heard the likes of that?
Where is he?

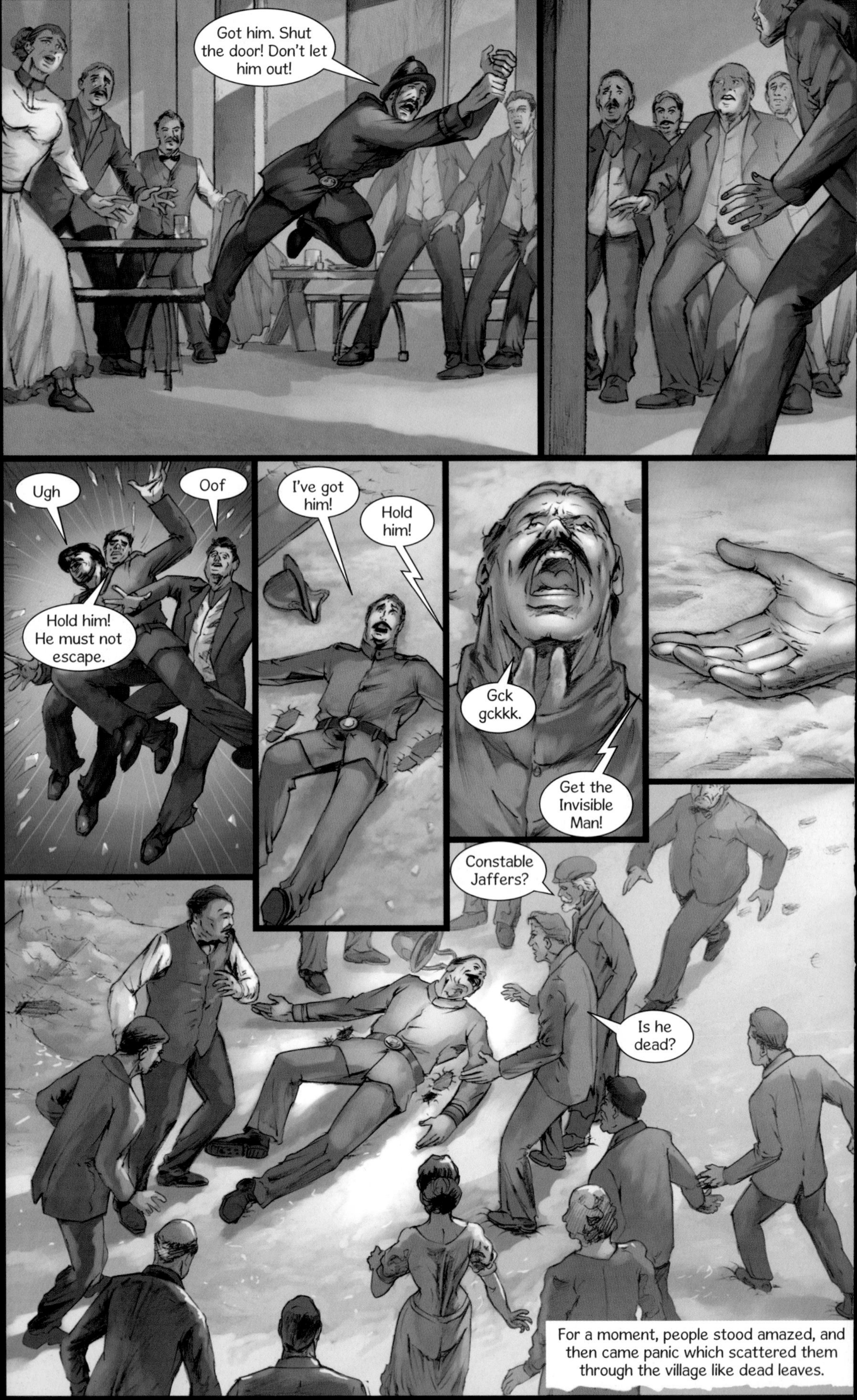
Got him. Shut the door! Don't let him out!
Ugh
Oof
Hold him! He must not escape.
I've got him!
Hold him!
Gck gckkk.
Get the Invisible Man!
Constable Jaffers?
Is he dead?
For a moment, people stood amazed, and then came panic which scattered them through the village like dead leaves.

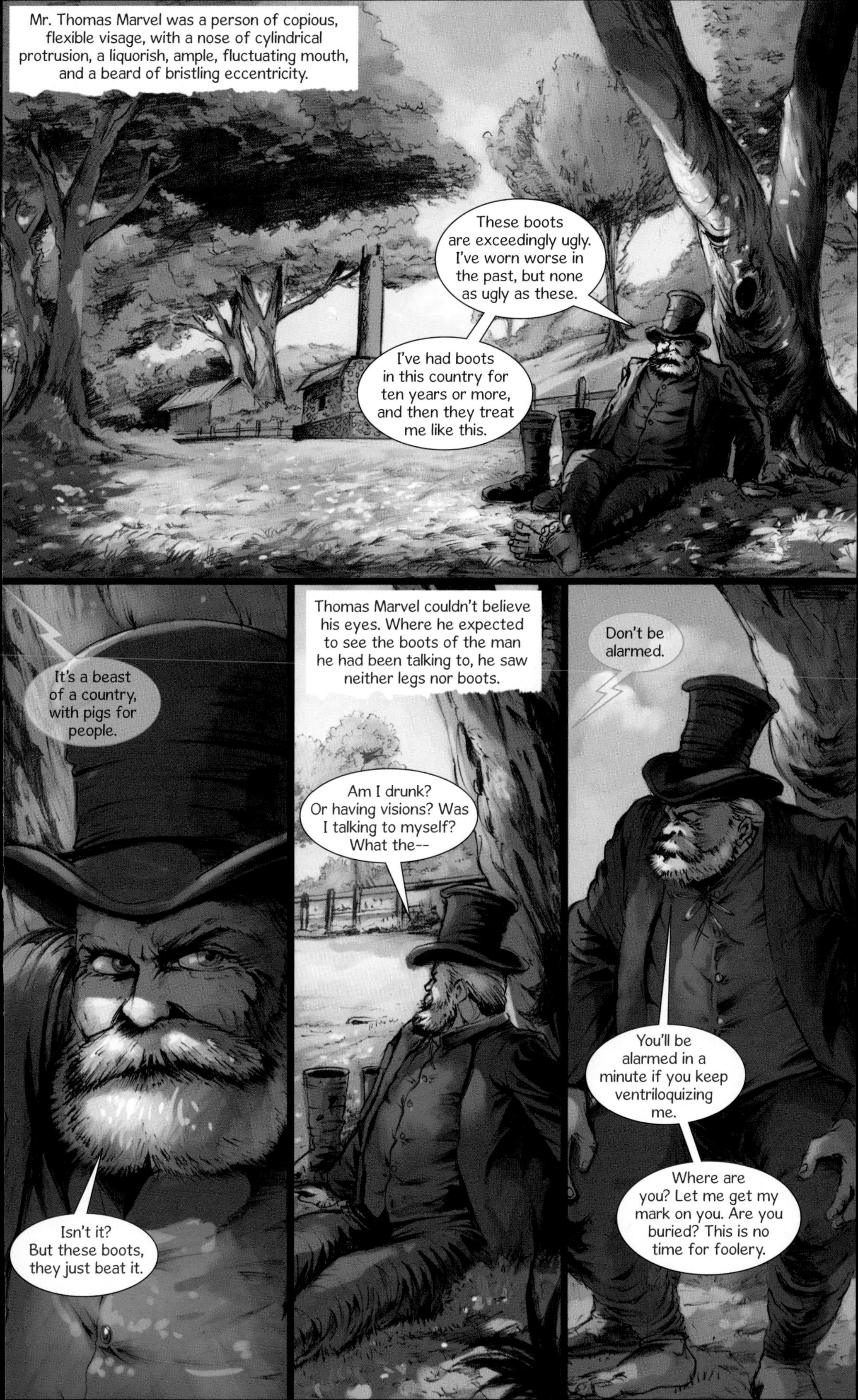
Mr. Thomas Marvel was a person of copious, flexible visage, with a nose of cylindrical protrusion, a liquorish, ample, fluctuating mouth, and a beard of bristling eccentricity.
These boots are exceedingly ugly. I've worn worse in the past, but none as ugly as these.
I've had boots in this country for ten years or more, and then they treat me like this.
It's a beast of a country, with pigs for people.
Isn't it? But these boots, they just beat it.
Thomas Marvel couldn't believe his eyes. Where he expected to see the boots of the man he had been talking to, he saw neither legs nor boots.
Am I drunk? Or having visions? Was I talking to myself? What the--
Don't be alarmed.
You'll be alarmed in a minute if you keep ventriloquizing me.
Where are you? Let me get my mark on you. Are you buried? This is no time for foolery.

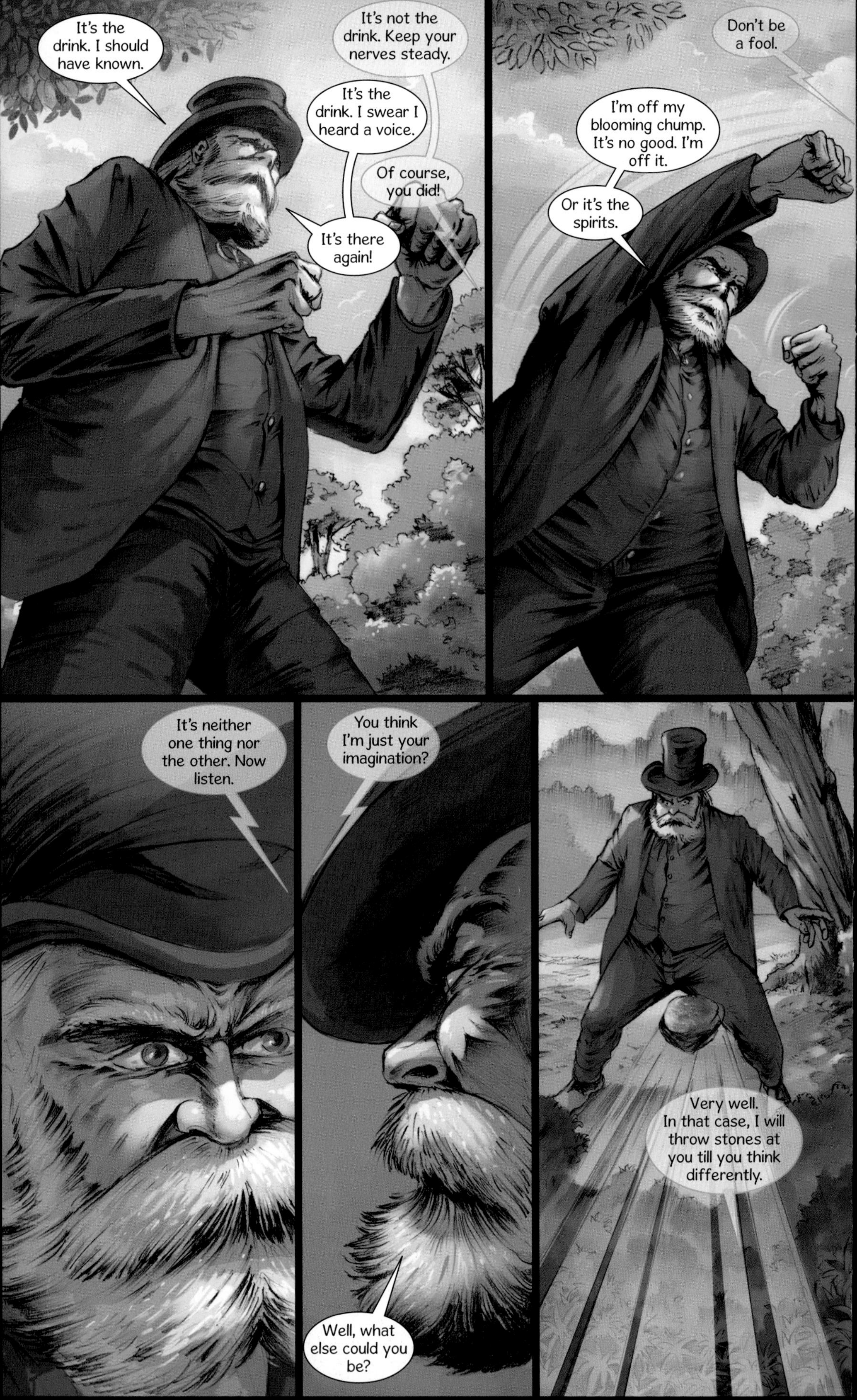
It's the drink. I should have known.
It's not the drink. Keep your nerves steady.
It's the drink. I swear I heard a voice.
Of course, you did!
It's there again!
Don't be a fool.
I'm off my blooming chump. It's no good. I'm off it.
Or it's the spirits.
It's neither one thing nor the other. Now listen.
You think I'm just your imagination?
Well, what else could you be?
Very well. In that case, I will throw stones at you till you think differently.

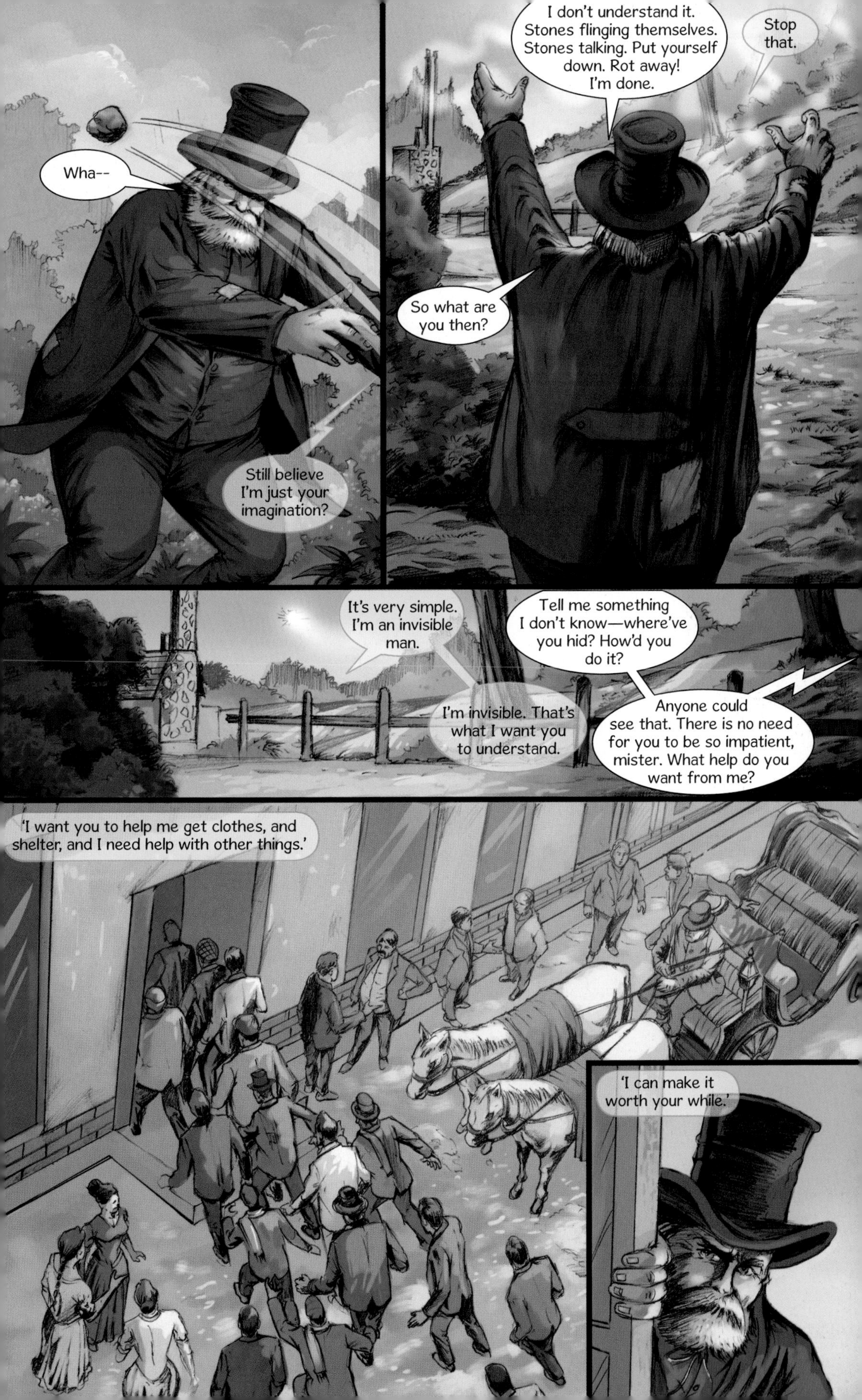
Wha--
Still believe I'm just your imagination?
I don't understand it. Stones flinging themselves. Stones talking. Put yourself down. Rot away! I'm done.
Stop that.
So what are you then?
It's very simple. I'm an invisible man.
I'm invisible. That's what I want you to understand.
Tell me something I don't know—where've you hid? How'd you do it?
Anyone could see that. There is no need for you to be so impatient, mister. What help do you want from me?
'I want you to help me get clothes, and shelter, and I need help with other things.'
'I can make it worth your while.'

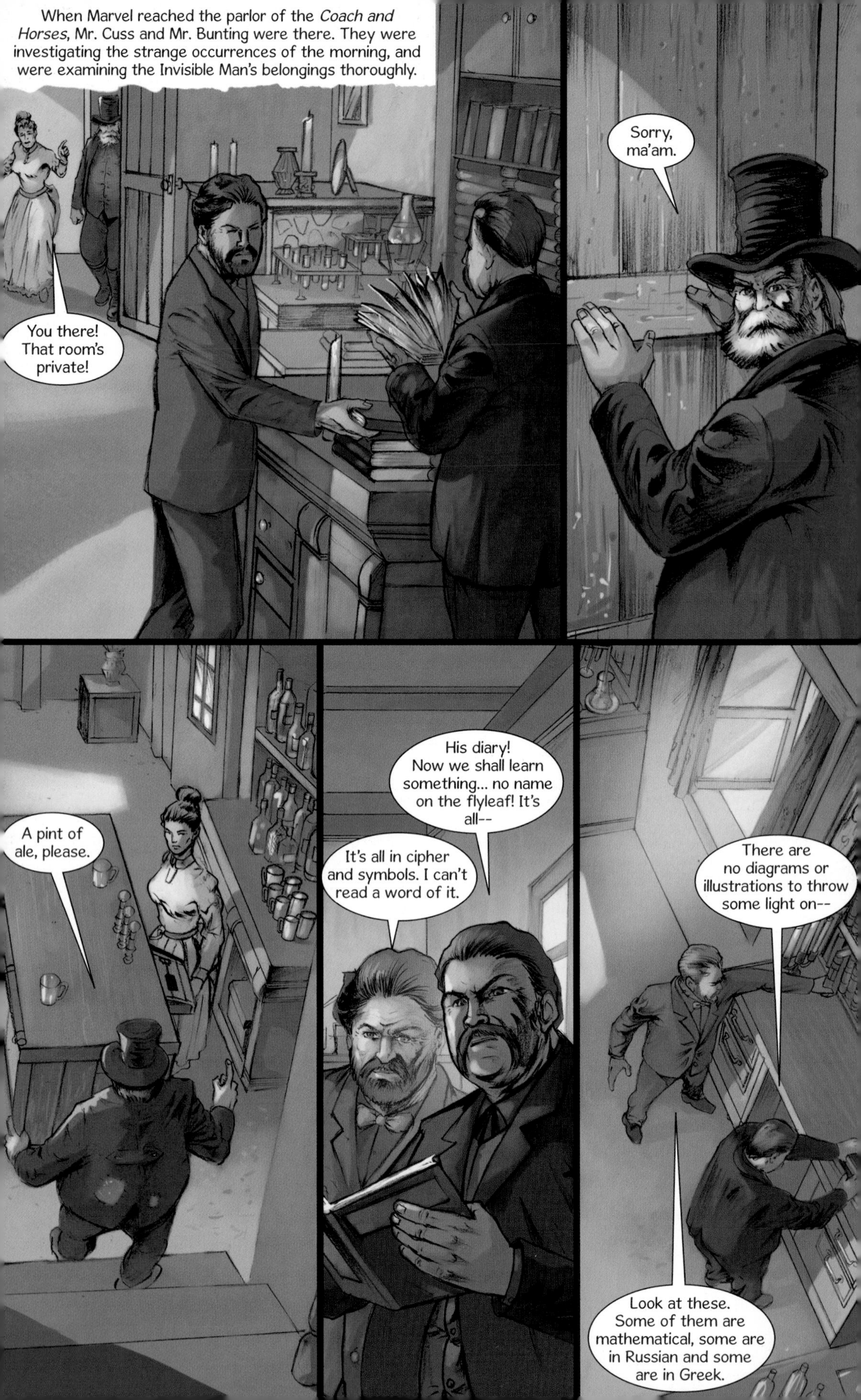
When Marvel reached the parlor of the *Coach and Horses*, Mr. Cuss and Mr. Bunting were there. They were investigating the strange occurrences of the morning, and were examining the Invisible Man's belongings thoroughly.
You there! That room's private!
Sorry, ma'am.
A pint of ale, please.
His diary! Now we shall learn something... no name on the flyleaf! It's all--
It's all in cipher and symbols. I can't read a word of it.
There are no diagrams or illustrations to throw some light on--
Look at these. Some of them are mathematical, some are in Russian and some are in Greek.

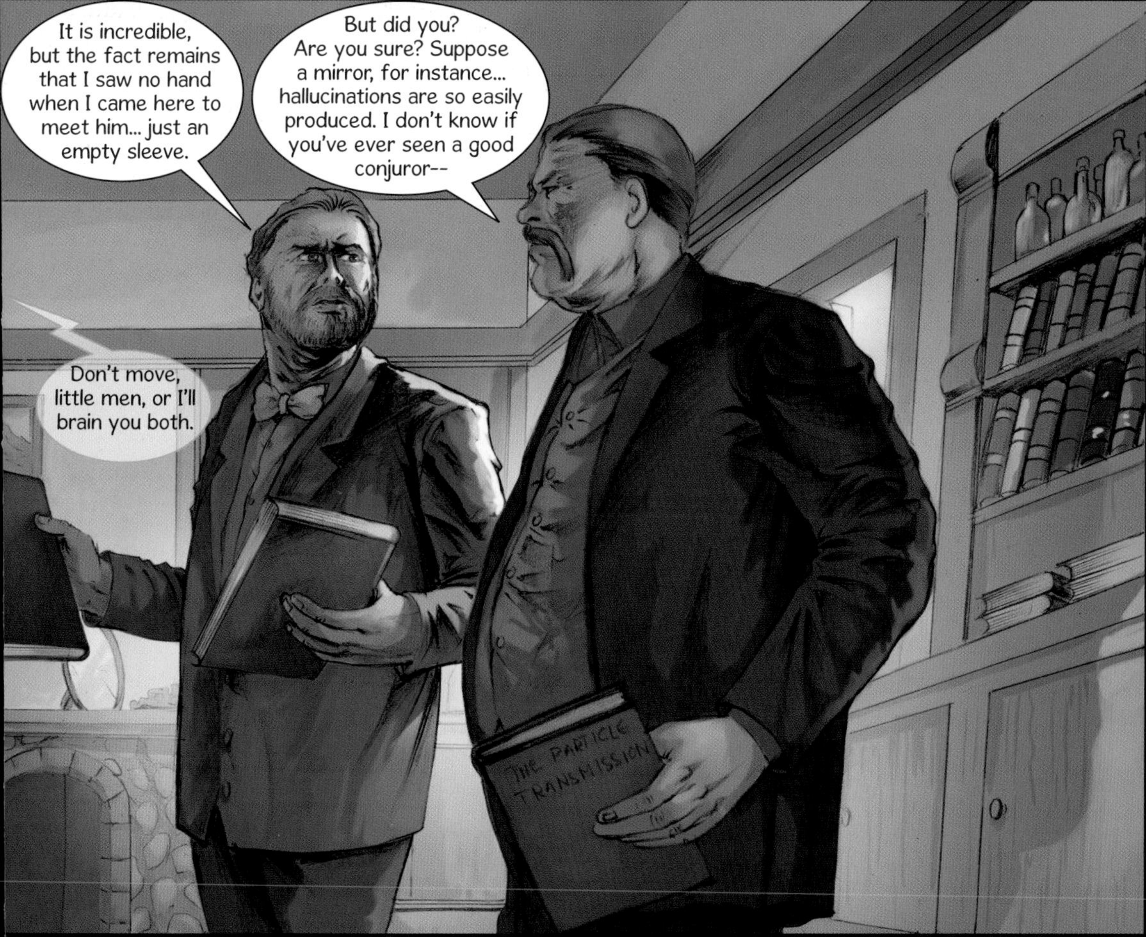
It is incredible, but the fact remains that I saw no hand when I came here to meet him... just an empty sleeve.
But did you? Are you sure? Suppose a mirror, for instance... hallucinations are so easily produced. I don't know if you've ever seen a good conjuror--
Don't move, little men, or I'll brain you both.
THE PARTICLE TRANSMISSION

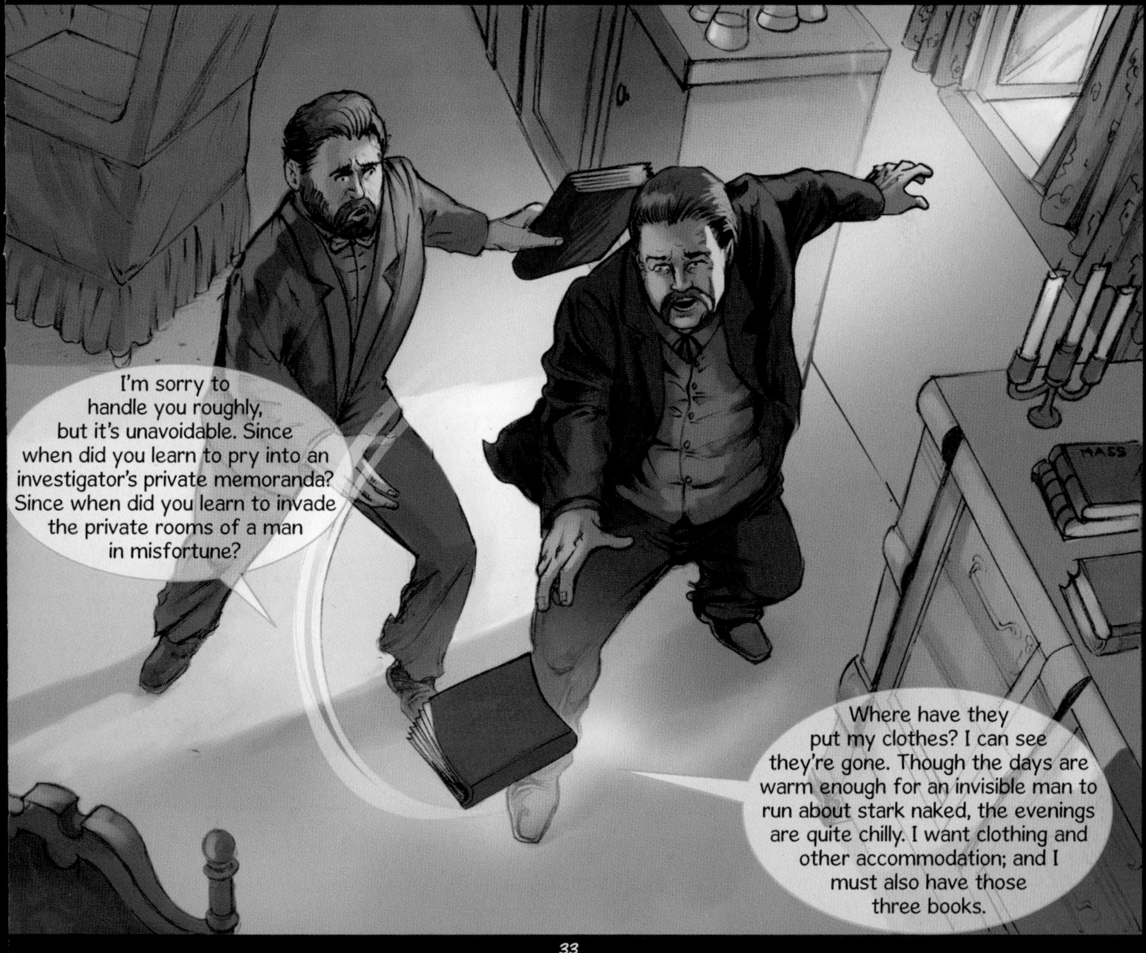
I'm sorry to handle you roughly, but it's unavoidable. Since when did you learn to pry into an investigator's private memoranda? Since when did you learn to invade the private rooms of a man in misfortune?
Where have they put my clothes? I can see they're gone. Though the days are warm enough for an invisible man to run about stark naked, the evenings are quite chilly. I want clothing and other accommodation; and I must also have those three books.

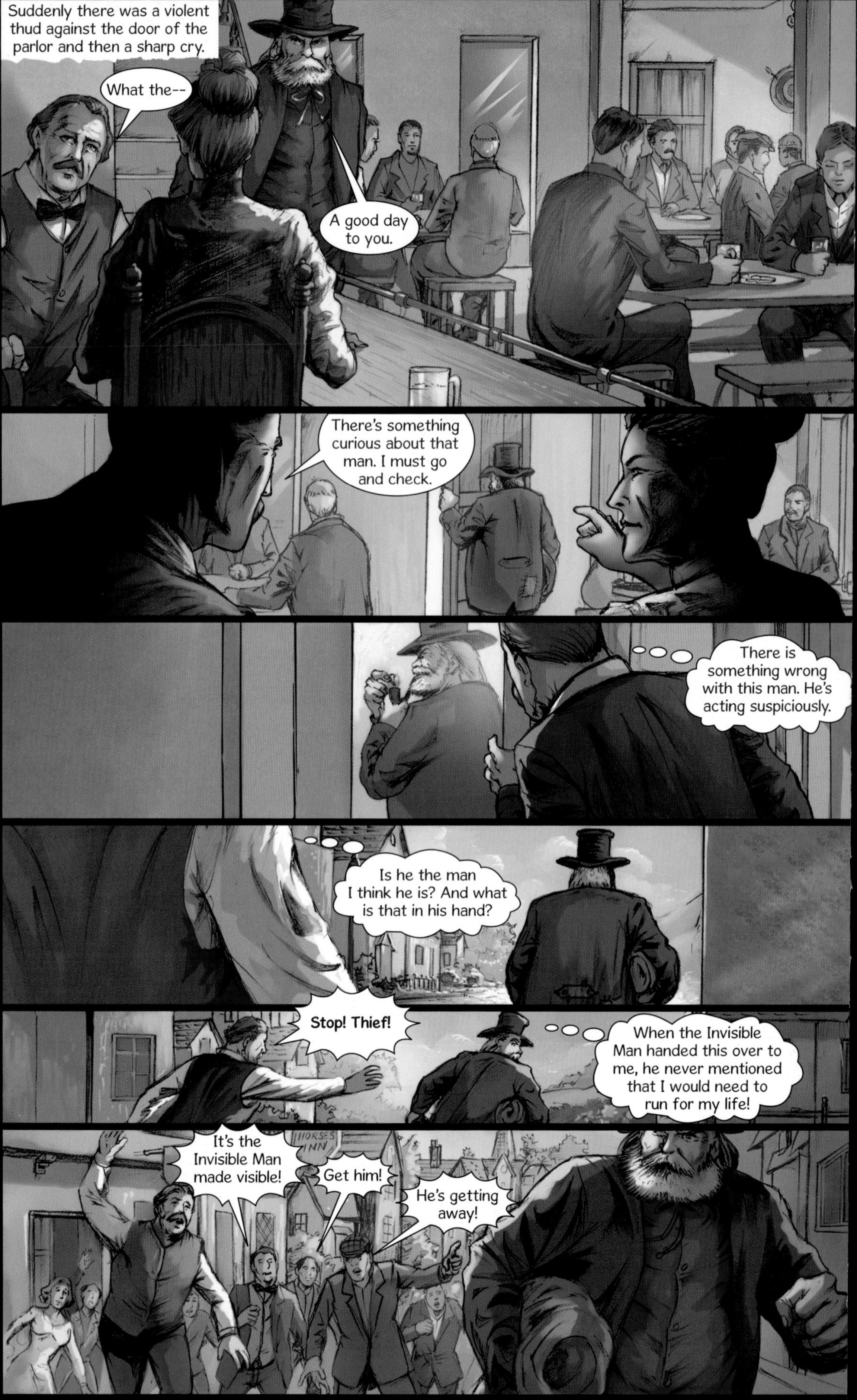
Suddenly there was a violent thud against the door of the parlor and then a sharp cry.
What the--
A good day to you.
There's something curious about that man. I must go and check.
There is something wrong with this man. He's acting suspiciously.
Is he the man I think he is? And what is that in his hand?
Stop! Thief!
When the Invisible Man handed this over to me, he never mentioned that I would need to run for my life!
It's the Invisible Man made visible!
Get him!
He's getting away!

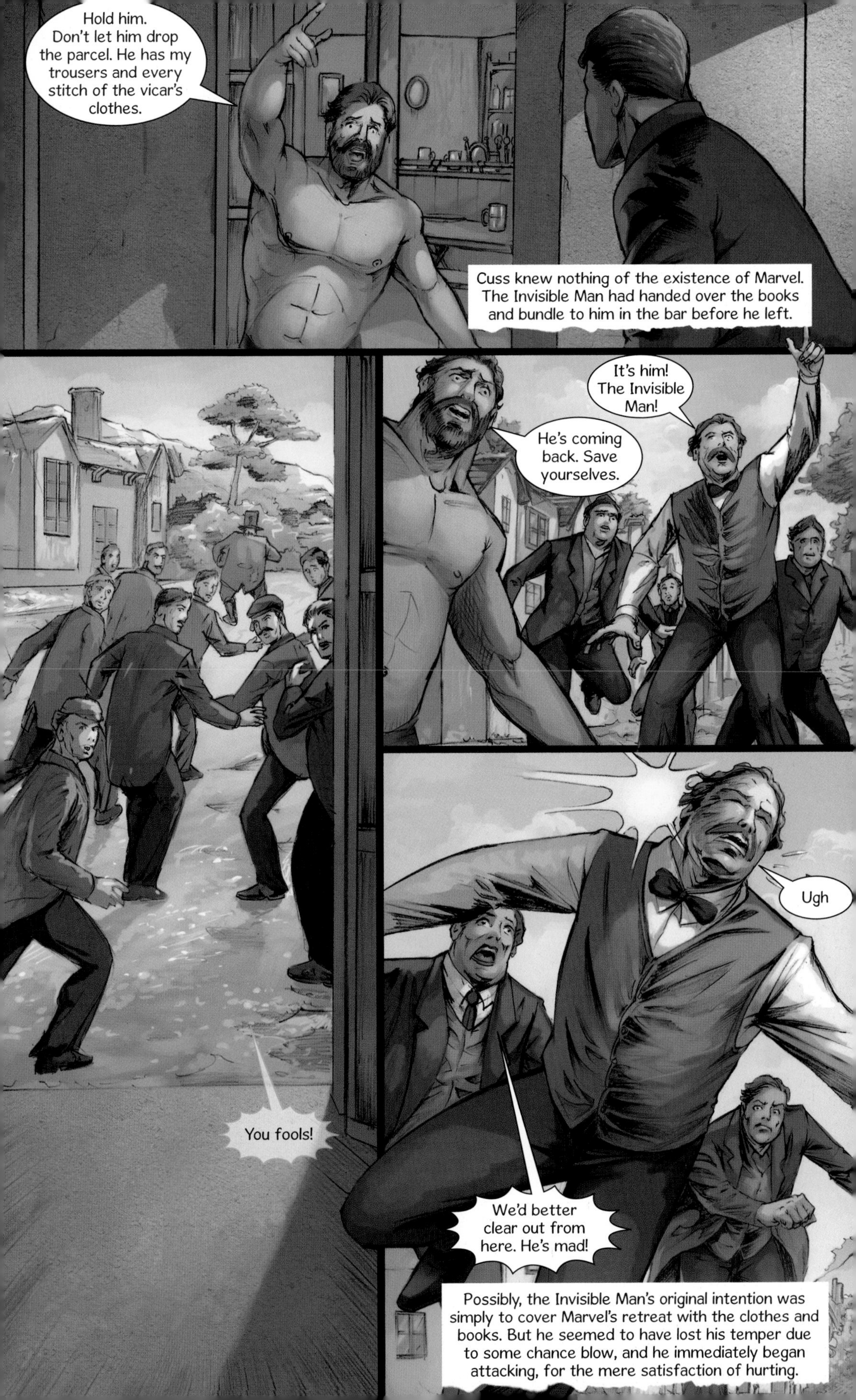

Hold him. Don't let him drop the parcel. He has my trousers and every stitch of the vicar's clothes.
Cuss knew nothing of the existence of Marvel. The Invisible Man had handed over the books and bundle to him in the bar before he left.
You fools!
It's him! The Invisible Man!
He's coming back. Save yourselves.
Ugh
We'd better clear out from here. He's mad!
Possibly, the Invisible Man's original intention was simply to cover Marvel's retreat with the clothes and books. But he seemed to have lost his temper due to some chance blow, and he immediately began attacking, for the mere satisfaction of hurting.

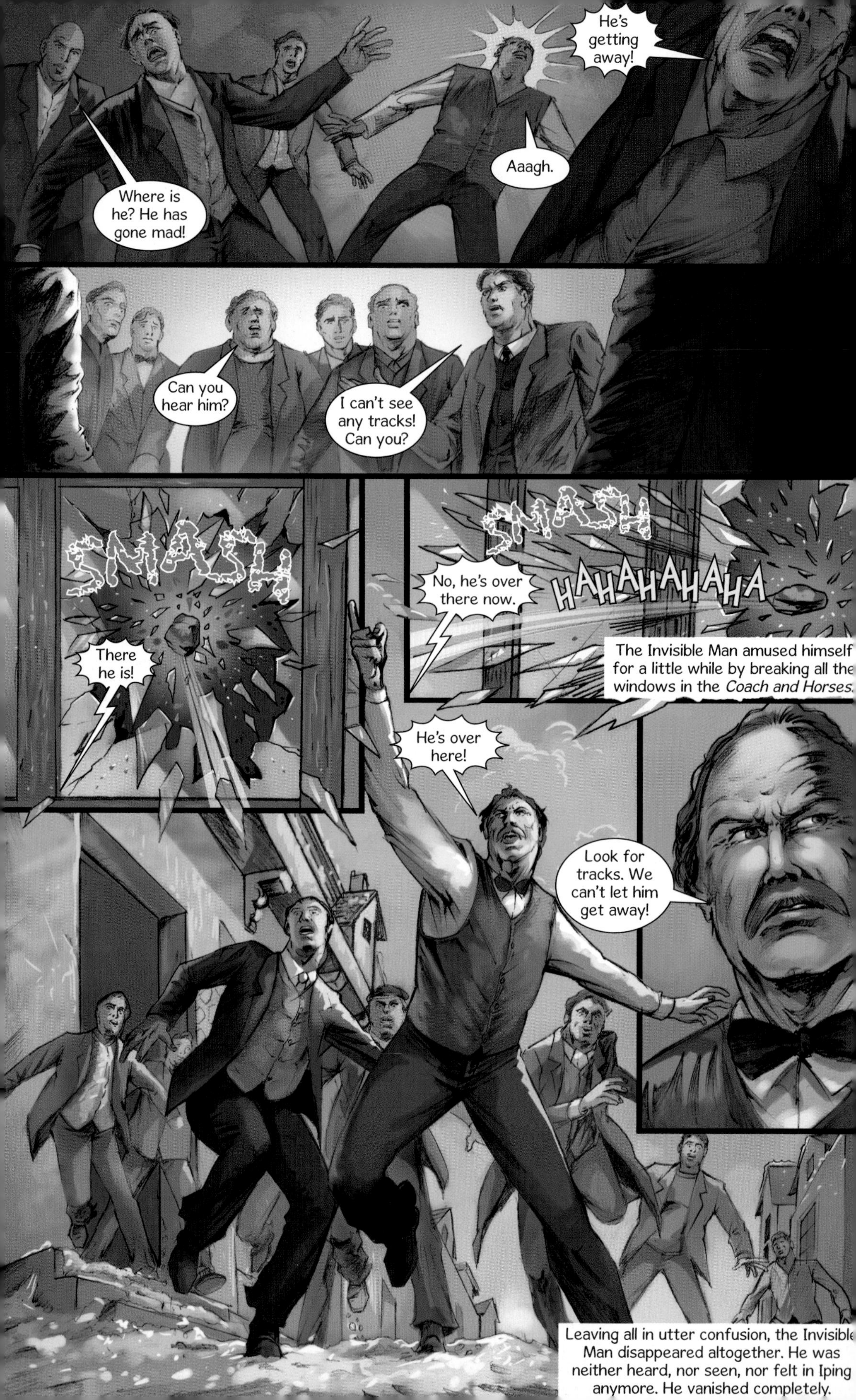
Where is he? He has gone mad!
Aaagh.
He's getting away!
Can you hear him?
I can't see any tracks! Can you?
SMASH
There he is!
SMASH
No, he's over there now.
HAHAHAHAHAHA
The Invisible Man amused himself for a little while by breaking all the windows in the *Coach and Horses*.
He's over here!
Look for tracks. We can't let him get away!
Leaving all in utter confusion, the Invisible Man disappeared altogether. He was neither heard, nor seen, nor felt in Iping anymore. He vanished completely.

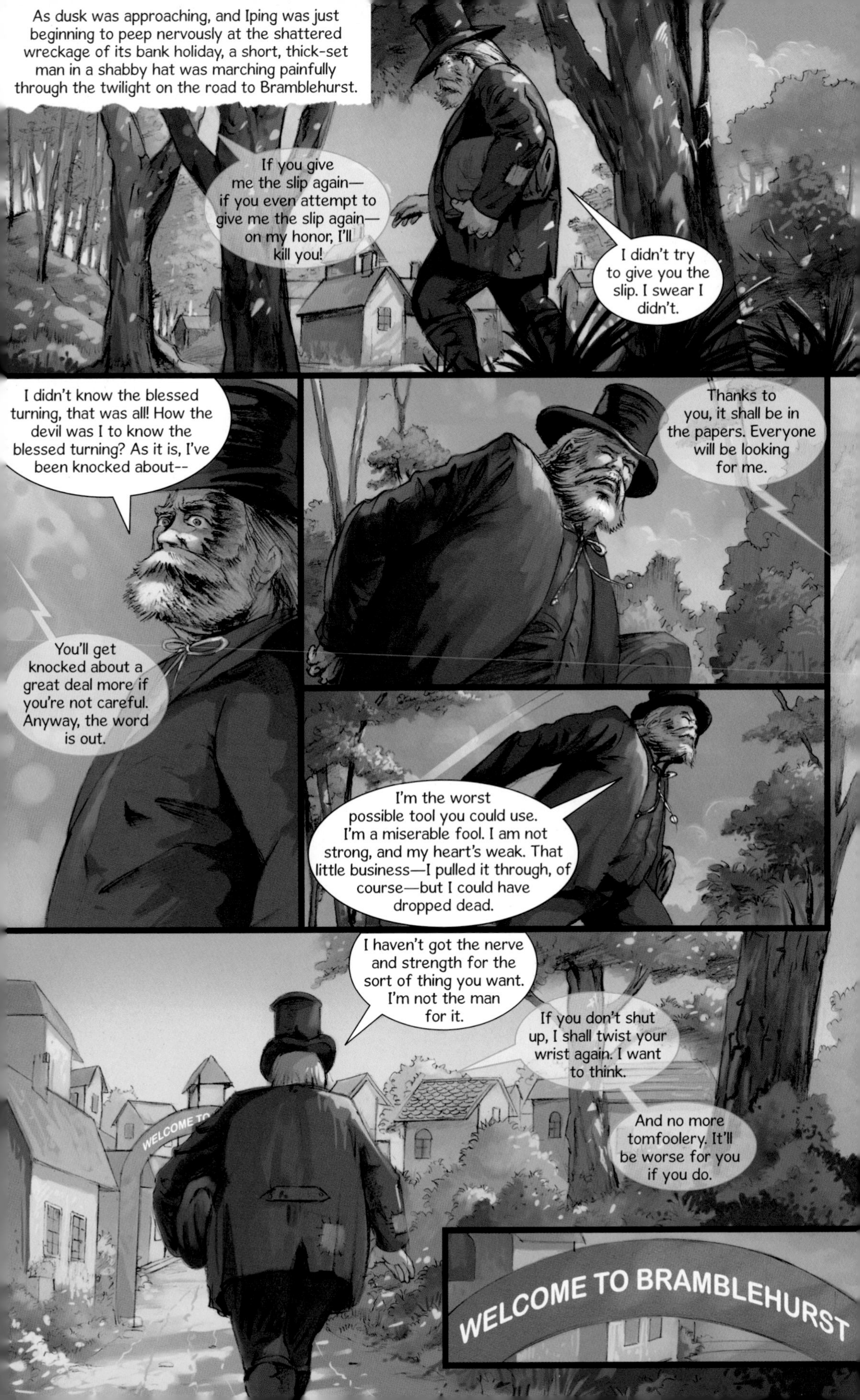
As dusk was approaching, and Iping was just beginning to peep nervously at the shattered wreckage of its bank holiday, a short, thick-set man in a shabby hat was marching painfully through the twilight on the road to Bramblehurst.
If you give me the slip again—if you even attempt to give me the slip again—on my honor, I'll kill you!
I didn't try to give you the slip. I swear I didn't.
I didn't know the blessed turning, that was all! How the devil was I to know the blessed turning? As it is, I've been knocked about--
You'll get knocked about a great deal more if you're not careful. Anyway, the word is out.
Thanks to you, it shall be in the papers. Everyone will be looking for me.
I'm the worst possible tool you could use. I'm a miserable fool. I am not strong, and my heart's weak. That little business—I pulled it through, of course—but I could have dropped dead.
I haven't got the nerve and strength for the sort of thing you want. I'm not the man for it.
If you don't shut up, I shall twist your wrist again. I want to think.
And no more tomfoolery. It'll be worse for you if you do.
WELCOME TO BRAMBLEHURST

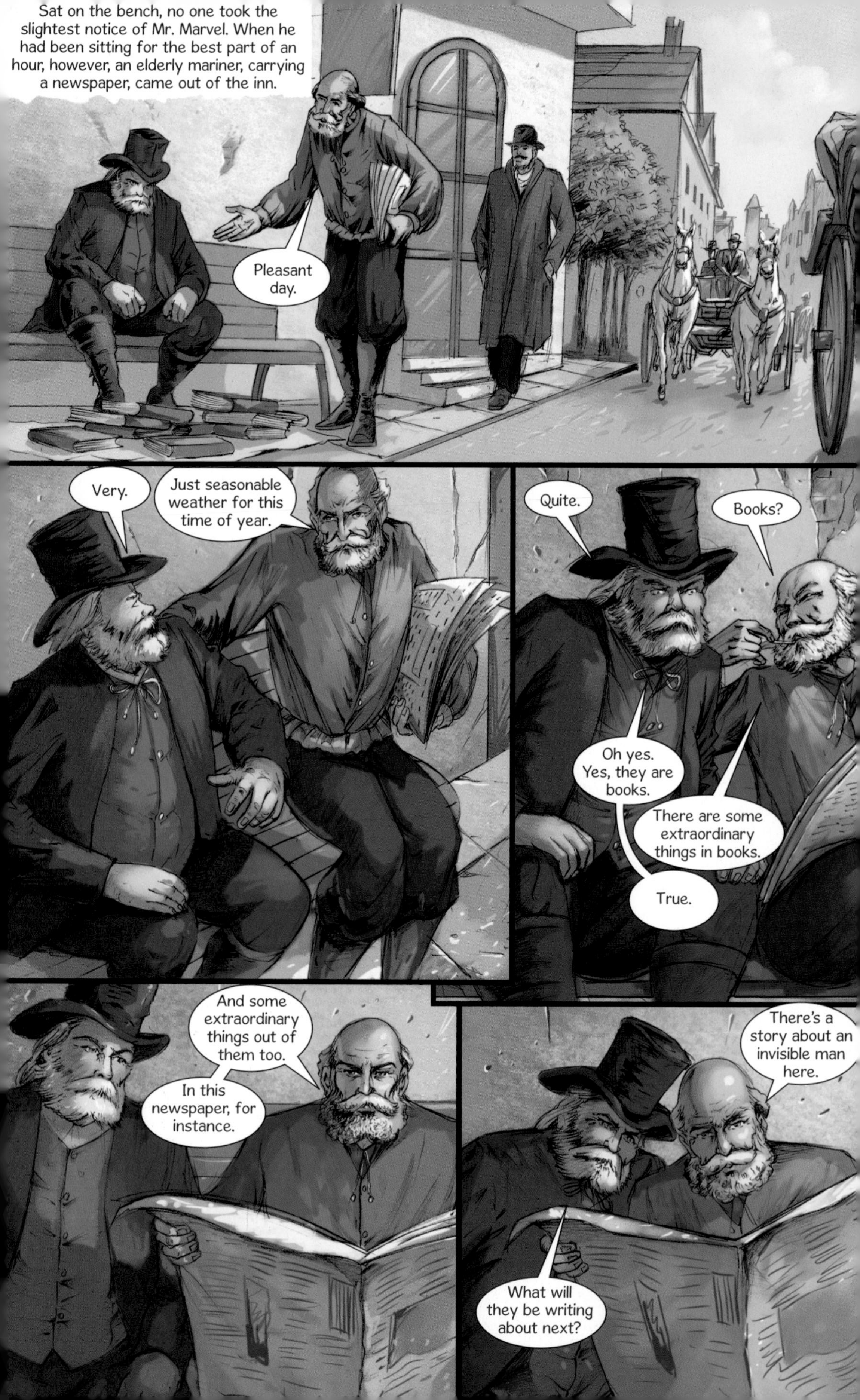
Sat on the bench, no one took the slightest notice of Mr. Marvel. When he had been sitting for the best part of an hour, however, an elderly mariner, carrying a newspaper, came out of the inn.
Pleasant day.
Very.
Just seasonable weather for this time of year.
Quite.
Books?
Oh yes. Yes, they are books.
There are some extraordinary things in books.
True.
And some extraordinary things out of them too.
In this newspaper, for instance.
There's a story about an invisible man here.
What will they be writing about next?

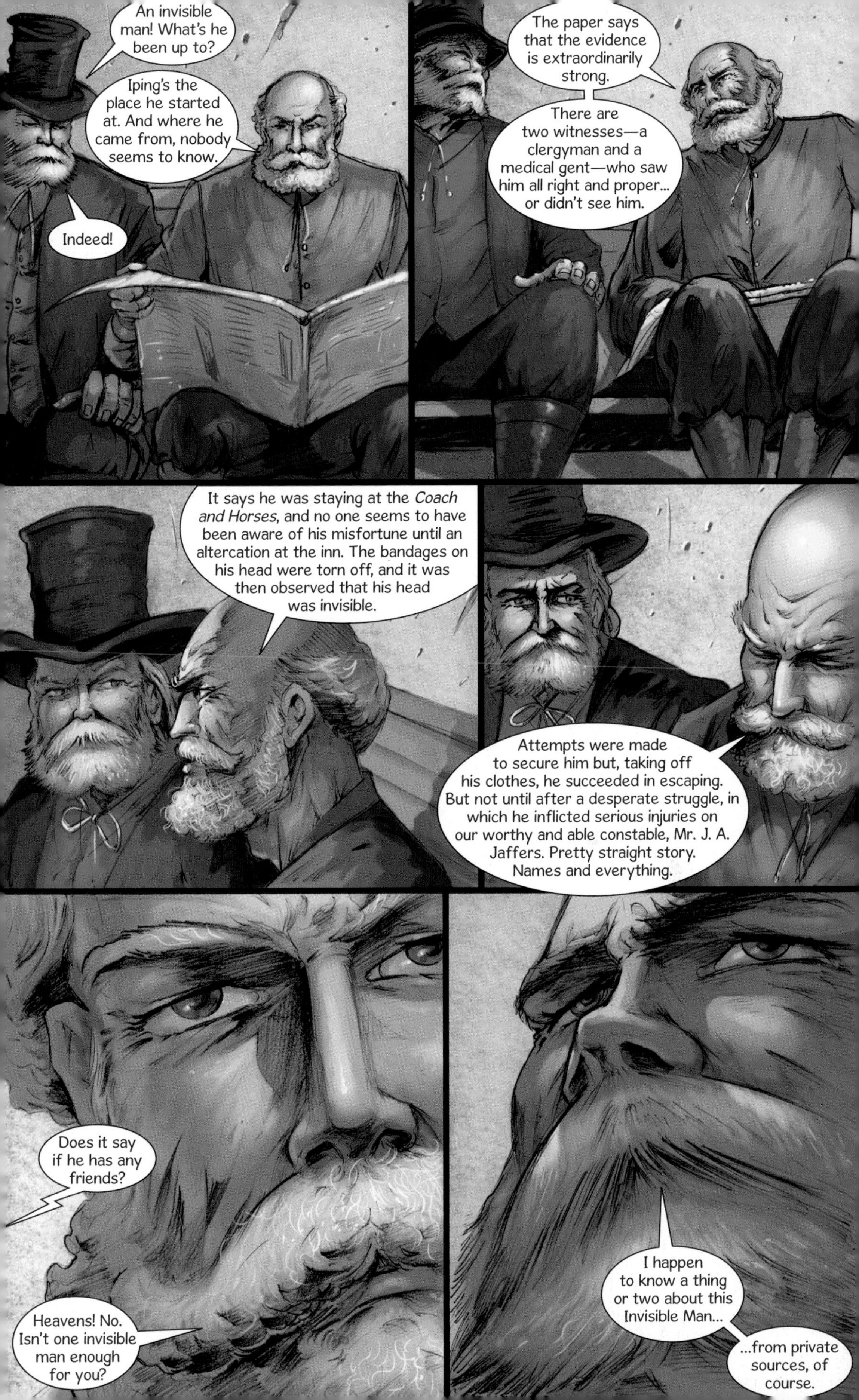
An invisible man! What's he been up to?
Iping's the place he started at. And where he came from, nobody seems to know.
Indeed!
The paper says that the evidence is extraordinarily strong.
There are two witnesses—a clergyman and a medical gent—who saw him all right and proper... or didn't see him.
It says he was staying at the *Coach and Horses*, and no one seems to have been aware of his misfortune until an altercation at the inn. The bandages on his head were torn off, and it was then observed that his head was invisible.
Attempts were made to secure him but, taking off his clothes, he succeeded in escaping. But not until after a desperate struggle, in which he inflicted serious injuries on our worthy and able constable, Mr. J. A. Jaffers. Pretty straight story. Names and everything.
Does it say if he has any friends?
Heavens! No. Isn't one invisible man enough for you?
I happen to know a thing or two about this Invisible Man...
...from private sources, of course.

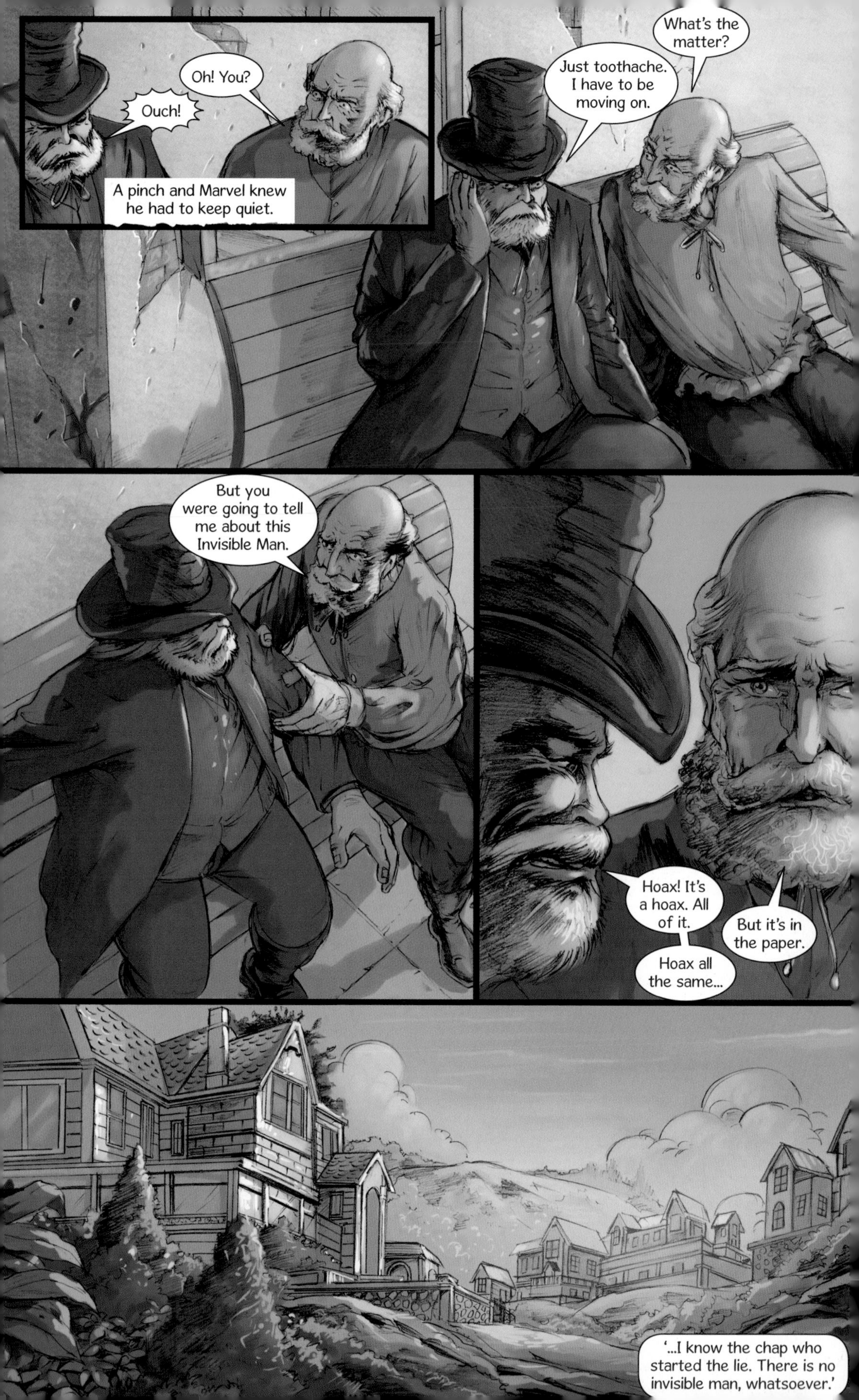
Ouch!
Oh! You?
A pinch and Marvel knew he had to keep quiet.
What's the matter?
Just toothache. I have to be moving on.
But you were going to tell me about this Invisible Man.
Hoax! It's a hoax. All of it.
But it's in the paper.
Hoax all the same...
'...I know the chap who started the lie. There is no invisible man, whatsoever.'

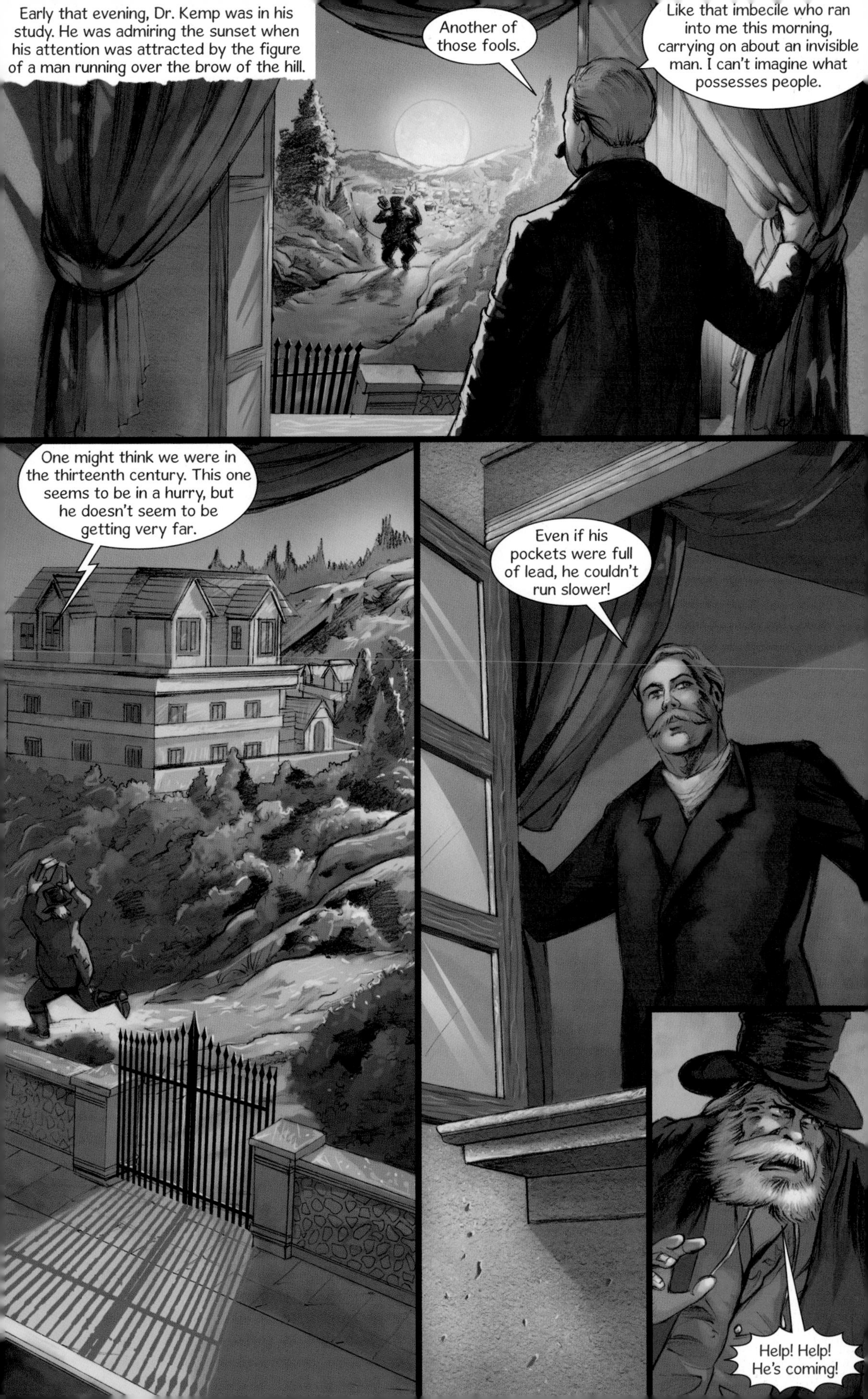
Early that evening, Dr. Kemp was in his study. He was admiring the sunset when his attention was attracted by the figure of a man running over the brow of the hill.
Another of those fools.
Like that imbecile who ran into me this morning, carrying on about an invisible man. I can't imagine what possesses people.
One might think we were in the thirteenth century. This one seems to be in a hurry, but he doesn't seem to be getting very far.
Even if his pockets were full of lead, he couldn't run slower!
Help! Help! He's coming!

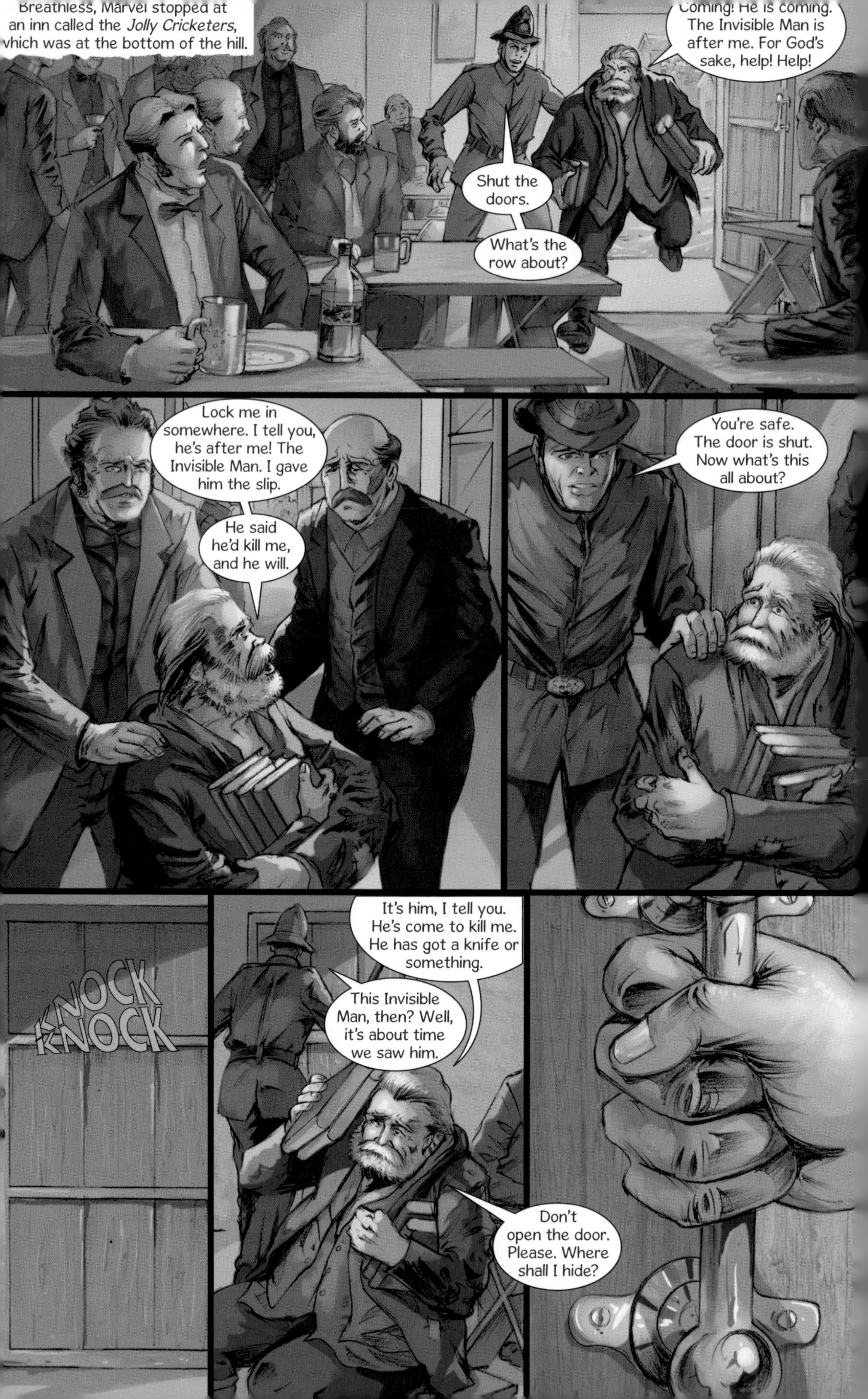

Breathless, Marvel stopped at an inn called the *Jolly Cricketers*, which was at the bottom of the hill.
Coming! He is coming. The Invisible Man is after me. For God's sake, help! Help!
Shut the doors.
What's the row about?
Lock me in somewhere. I tell you, he's after me! The Invisible Man. I gave him the slip.
He said he'd kill me, and he will.
You're safe. The door is shut. Now what's this all about?
KNOCK KNOCK
It's him, I tell you. He's come to kill me. He has got a knife or something.
This Invisible Man, then? Well, it's about time we saw him.
Don't open the door. Please. Where shall I hide?

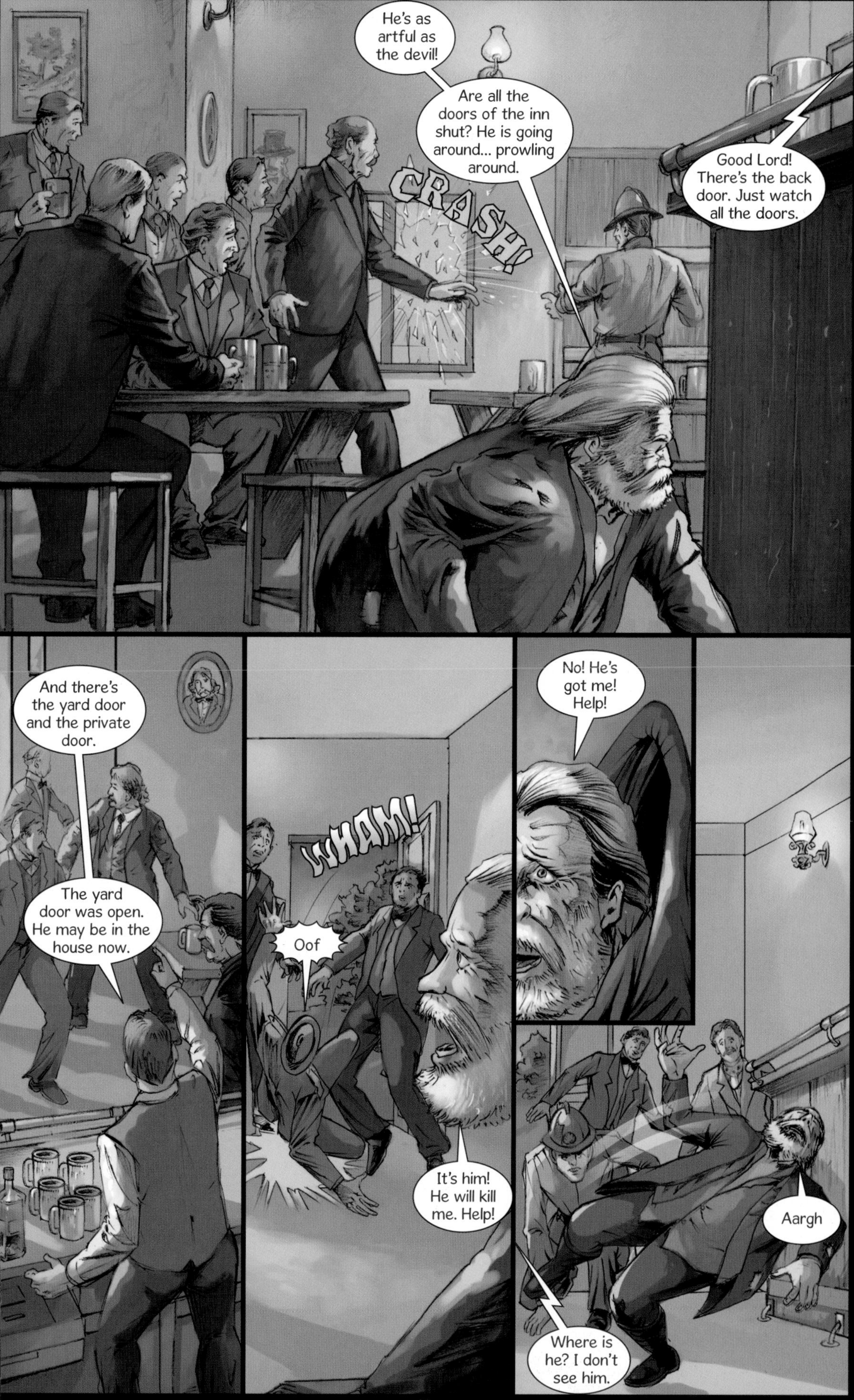

He's as artful as the devil!
Are all the doors of the inn shut? He is going around... prowling around.
CRASH!
Good Lord! There's the back door. Just watch all the doors.
And there's the yard door and the private door.
The yard door was open. He may be in the house now.
WHAM!
Oof
It's him! He will kill me. Help!
No! He's got me! Help!
Aargh
Where is he? I don't see him.

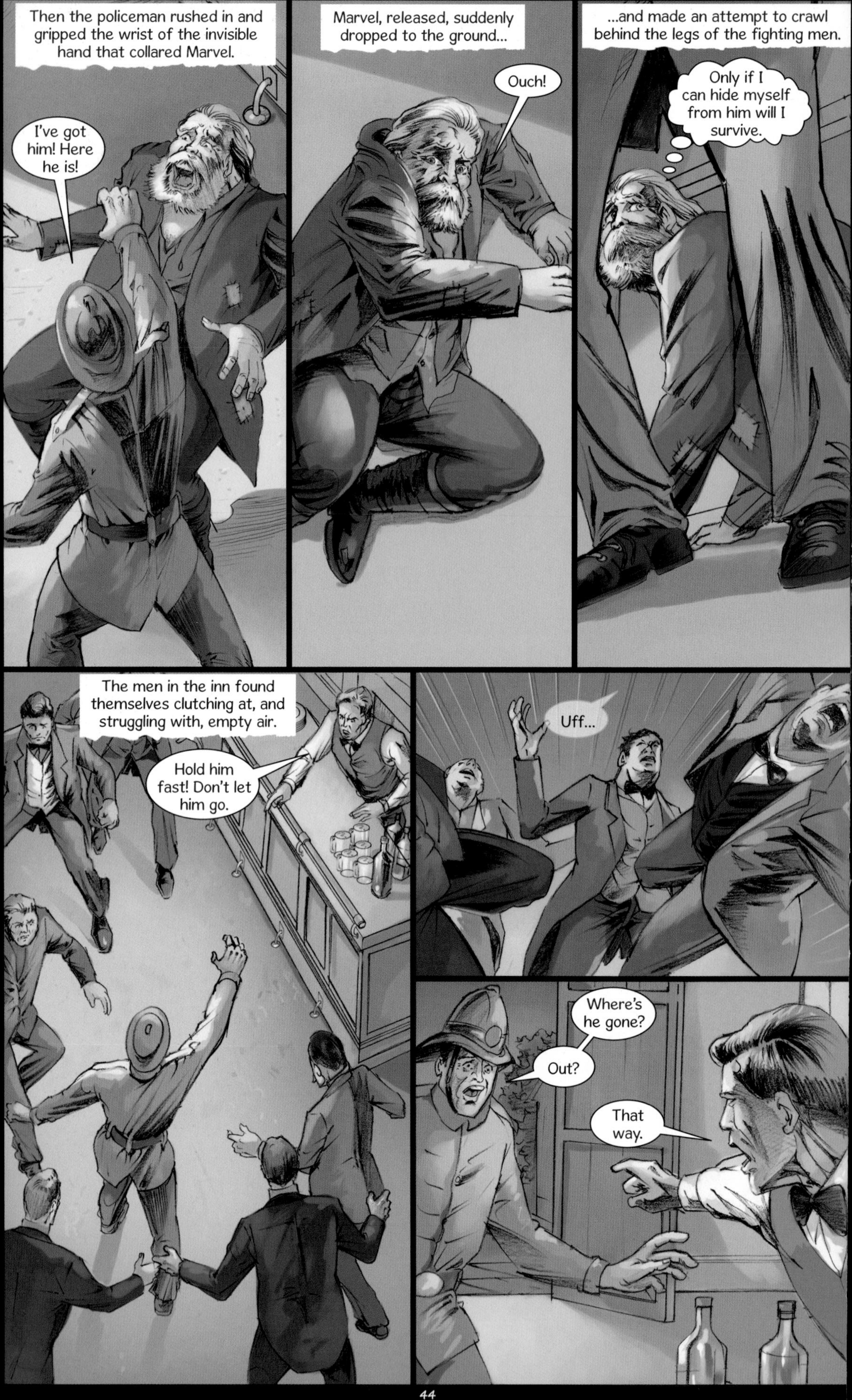
Then the policeman rushed in and gripped the wrist of the invisible hand that collared Marvel.
I've got him! Here he is!
Marvel, released, suddenly dropped to the ground...
Ouch!
...and made an attempt to crawl behind the legs of the fighting men.
Only if I can hide myself from him will I survive.
The men in the inn found themselves clutching at, and struggling with, empty air.
Hold him fast! Don't let him go.
Uff...
Where's he gone?
Out?
That way.

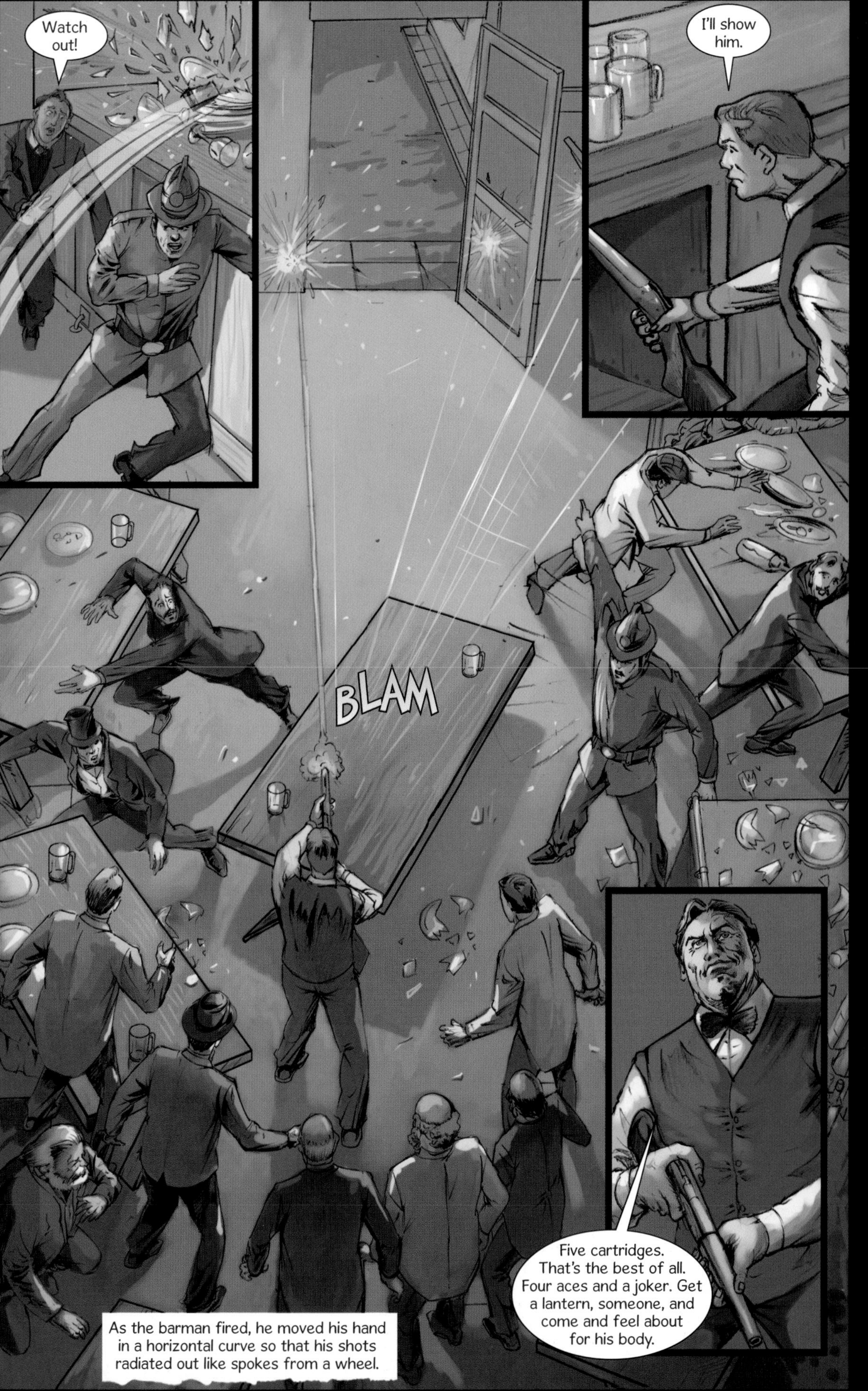

Watch out!
I'll show him.
BLAM
As the barman fired, he moved his hand in a horizontal curve so that his shots radiated out like spokes from a wheel.
Five cartridges. That's the best of all. Four aces and a joker. Get a lantern, someone, and come and feel about for his body.

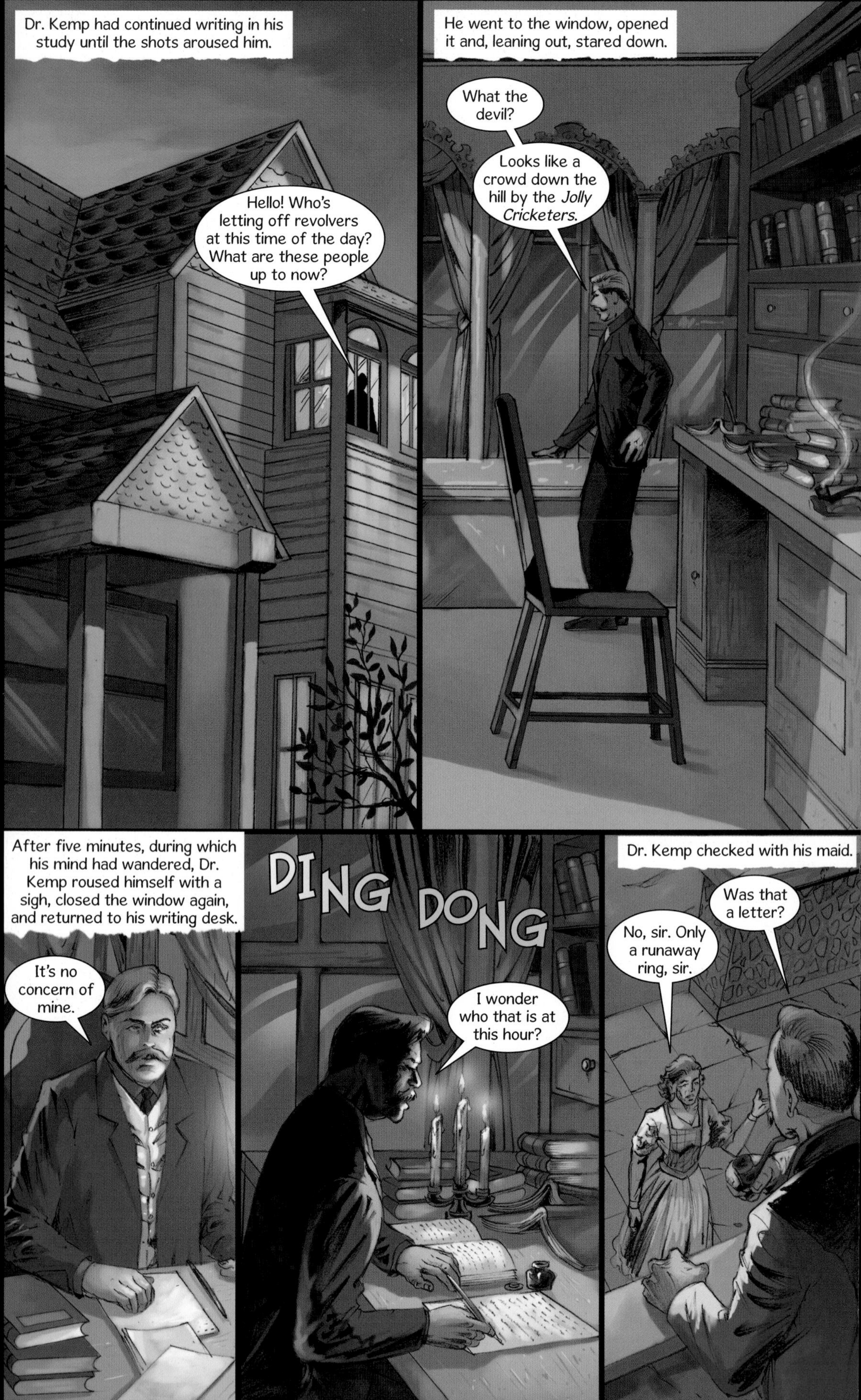
Dr. Kemp had continued writing in his study until the shots aroused him.
Hello! Who's letting off revolvers at this time of the day? What are these people up to now?
He went to the window, opened it and, leaning out, stared down.
What the devil?
Looks like a crowd down the hill by the *Jolly Cricketers*.
After five minutes, during which his mind had wandered, Dr. Kemp roused himself with a sigh, closed the window again, and returned to his writing desk.
It's no concern of mine.
DING DONG
I wonder who that is at this hour?
Dr. Kemp checked with his maid.
Was that a letter?
No, sir. Only a runaway ring, sir.

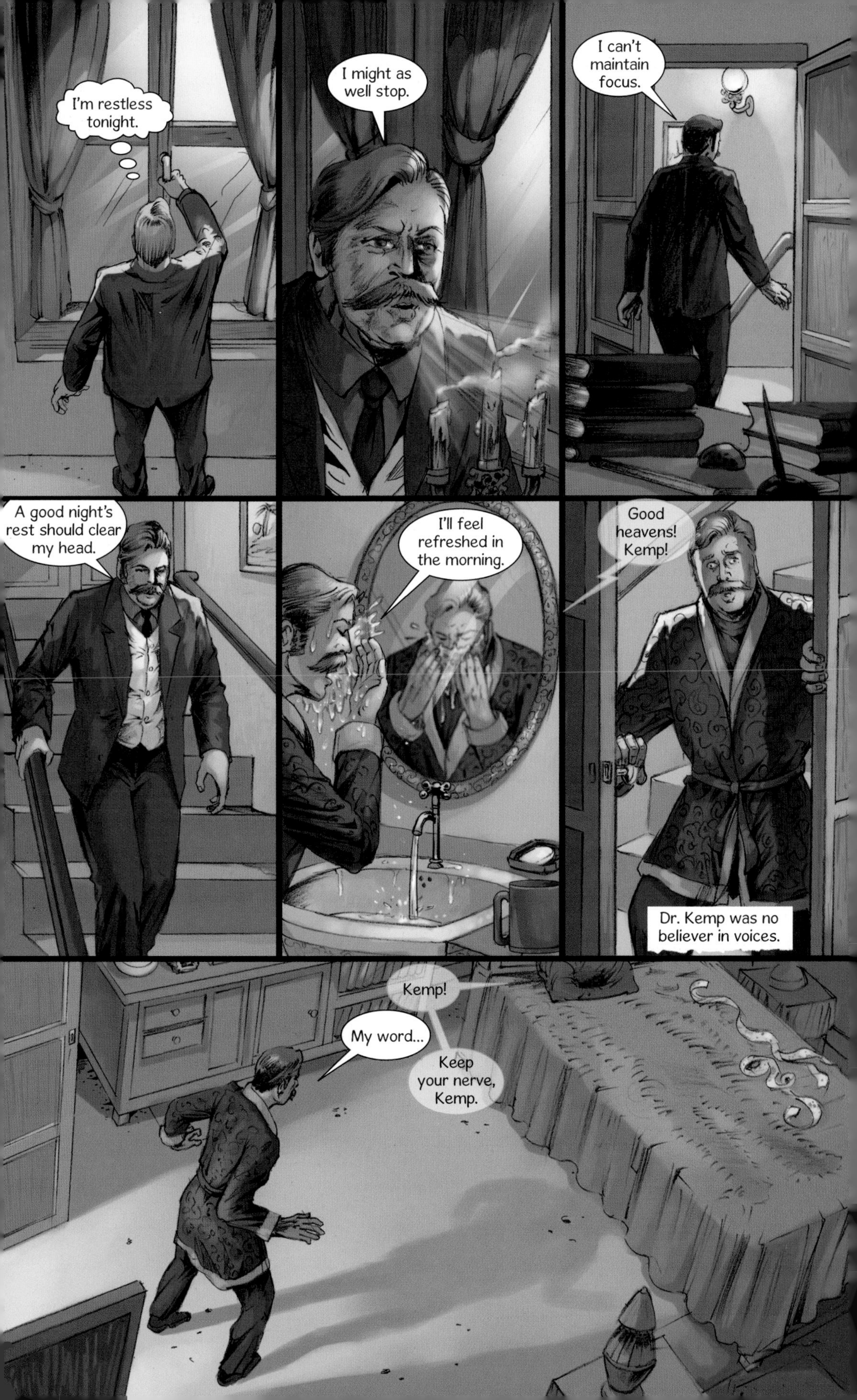
I'm restless tonight.
I might as well stop.
I can't maintain focus.
A good night's rest should clear my head.
I'll feel refreshed in the morning.
Good heavens! Kemp!
Dr. Kemp was no believer in voices.
Kemp!
My word...
Keep your nerve, Kemp.

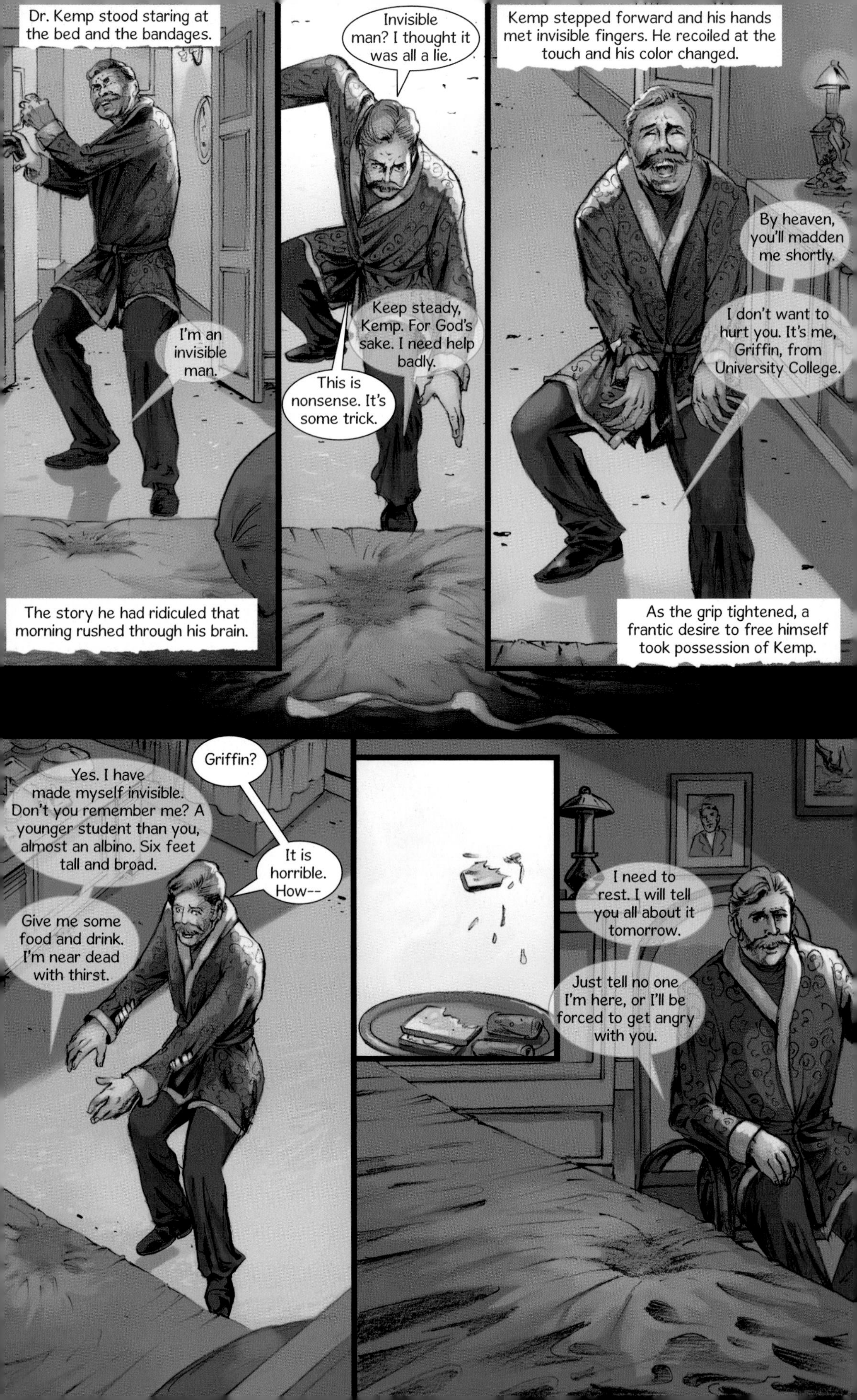
Dr. Kemp stood staring at the bed and the bandages.
I'm an invisible man.
The story he had ridiculed that morning rushed through his brain.
Invisible man? I thought it was all a lie.
Keep steady, Kemp. For God's sake. I need help badly.
This is nonsense. It's some trick.
Kemp stepped forward and his hands met invisible fingers. He recoiled at the touch and his color changed.
By heaven, you'll madden me shortly.
I don't want to hurt you. It's me, Griffin, from University College.
As the grip tightened, a frantic desire to free himself took possession of Kemp.
Griffin?
Yes. I have made myself invisible. Don't you remember me? A younger student than you, almost an albino. Six feet tall and broad.
It is horrible. How--
Give me some food and drink. I'm near dead with thirst.
I need to rest. I will tell you all about it tomorrow.
Just tell no one I'm here, or I'll be forced to get angry with you.

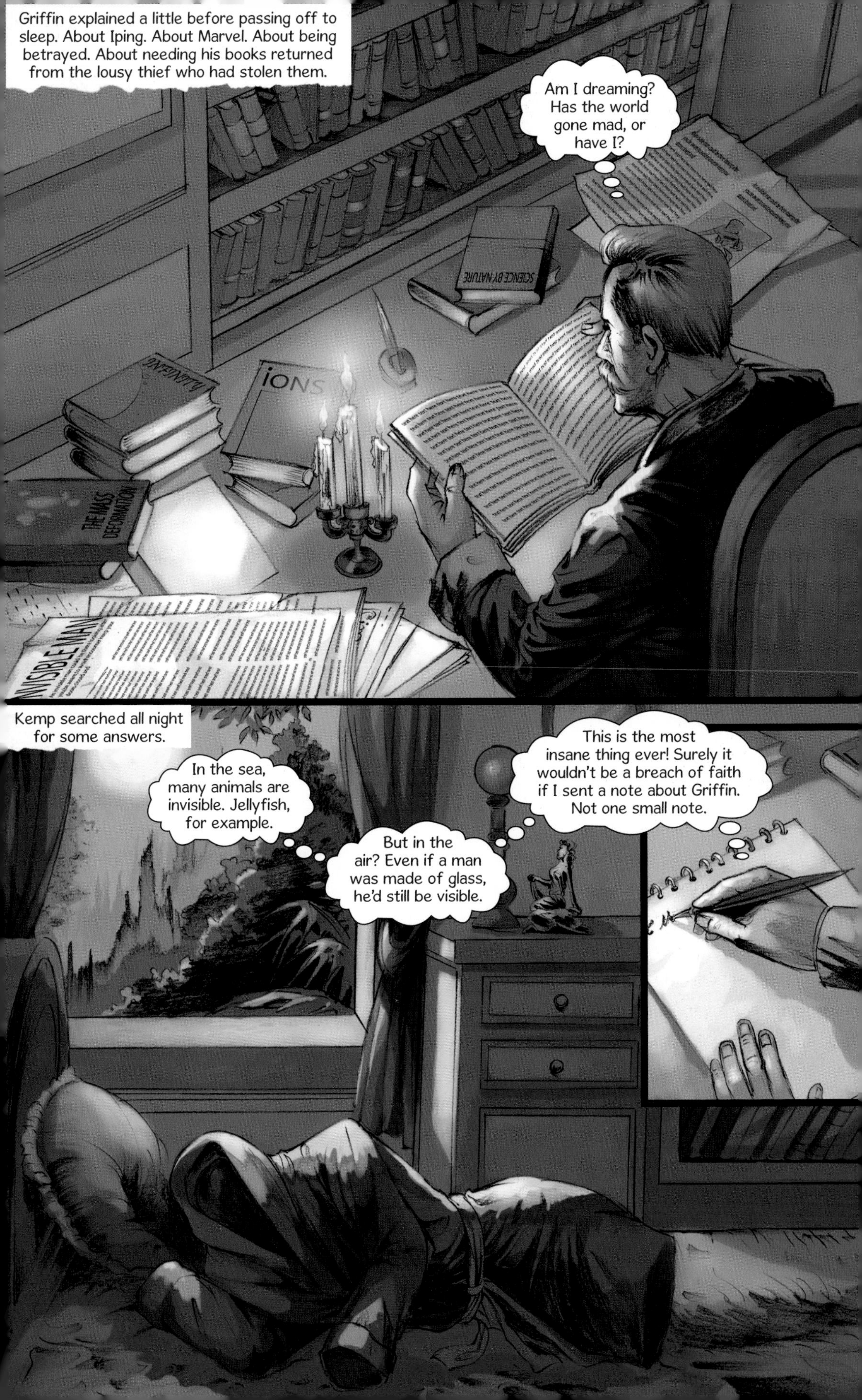
Griffin explained a little before passing off to sleep. About Iping. About Marvel. About being betrayed. About needing his books returned from the lousy thief who had stolen them.
Am I dreaming? Has the world gone mad, or have I?
SCIENCE BY NATURE
iONS
THE MASS DEFORMATION
INVISIBLE MAN
Kemp searched all night for some answers.
In the sea, many animals are invisible. Jellyfish, for example.
But in the air? Even if a man was made of glass, he'd still be visible.
This is the most insane thing ever! Surely it wouldn't be a breach of faith if I sent a note about Griffin. Not one small note.

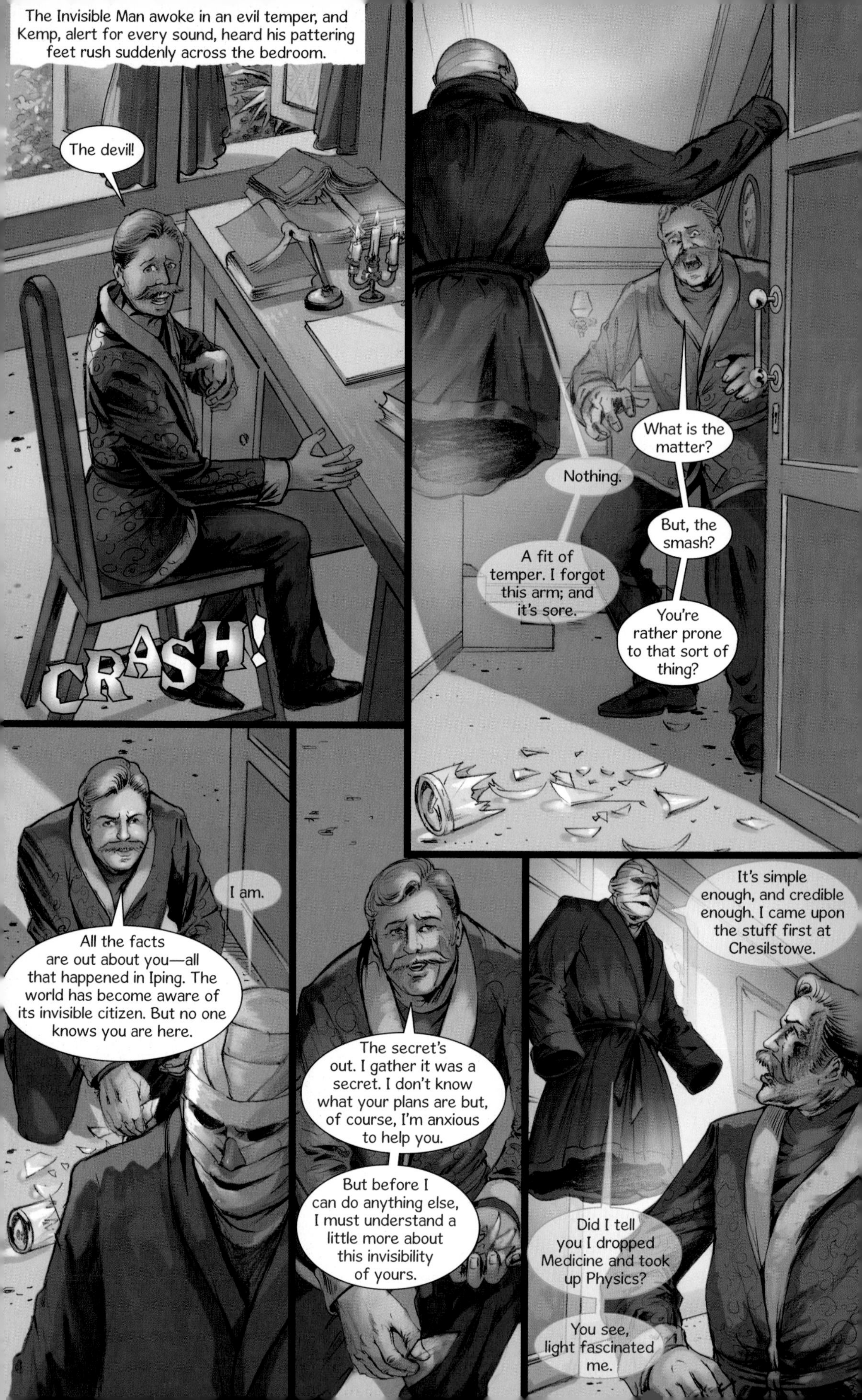

The Invisible Man awoke in an evil temper, and Kemp, alert for every sound, heard his pattering feet rush suddenly across the bedroom.
The devil!
CRASH!
What is the matter?
Nothing.
But, the smash?
A fit of temper. I forgot this arm; and it's sore.
You're rather prone to that sort of thing?
I am.
All the facts are out about you—all that happened in Iping. The world has become aware of its invisible citizen. But no one knows you are here.
The secret's out. I gather it was a secret. I don't know what your plans are but, of course, I'm anxious to help you.
But before I can do anything else, I must understand a little more about this invisibility of yours.
It's simple enough, and credible enough. I came upon the stuff first at Chesilstowe.
Did I tell you I dropped Medicine and took up Physics?
You see, light fascinated me.

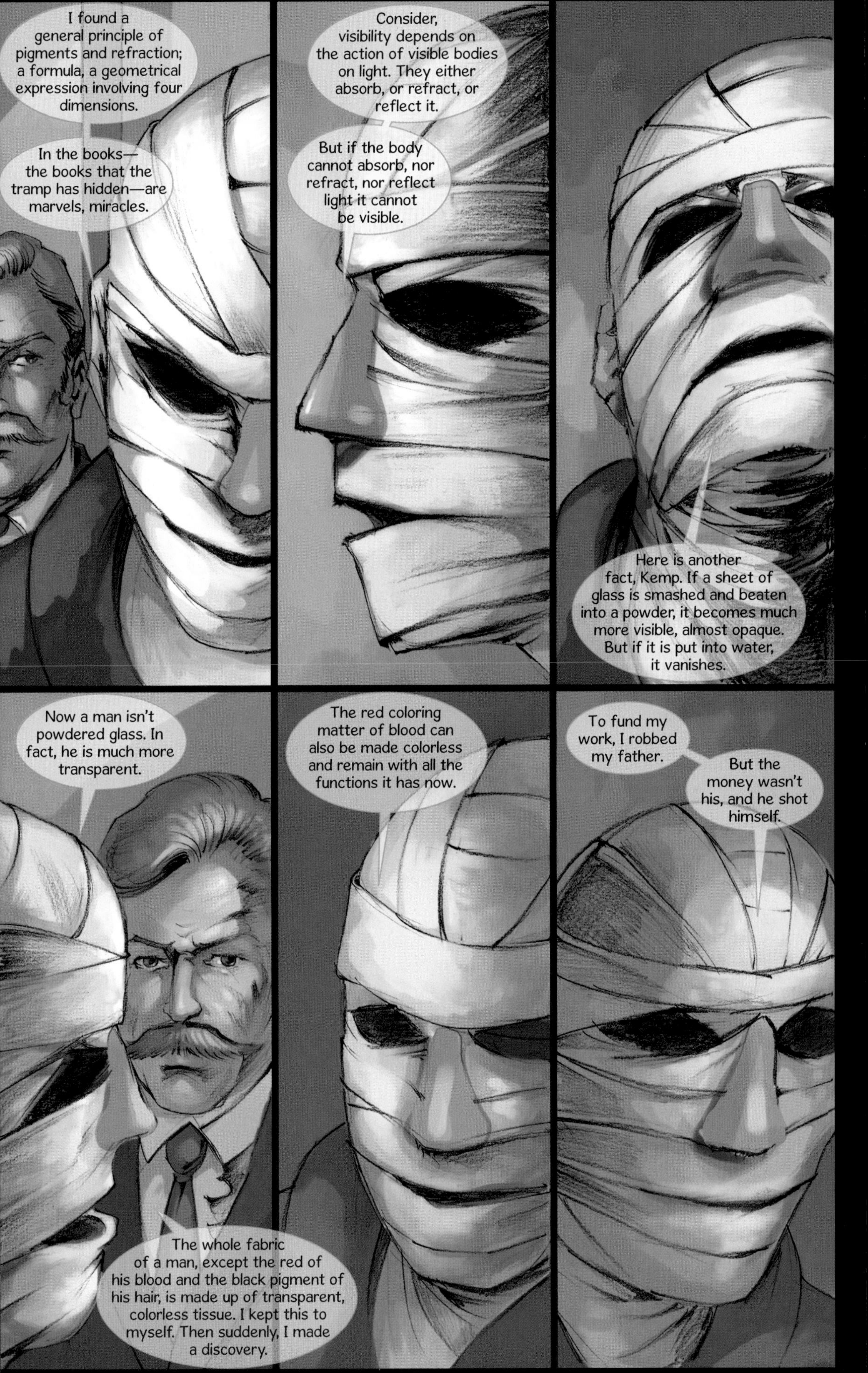
I found a general principle of pigments and refraction; a formula, a geometrical expression involving four dimensions.
In the books—the books that the tramp has hidden—are marvels, miracles.
Consider, visibility depends on the action of visible bodies on light. They either absorb, or refract, or reflect it.
But if the body cannot absorb, nor refract, nor reflect light it cannot be visible.
Here is another fact, Kemp. If a sheet of glass is smashed and beaten into a powder, it becomes much more visible, almost opaque. But if it is put into water, it vanishes.
Now a man isn't powdered glass. In fact, he is much more transparent.
The whole fabric of a man, except the red of his blood and the black pigment of his hair, is made up of transparent, colorless tissue. I kept this to myself. Then suddenly, I made a discovery.
The red coloring matter of blood can also be made colorless and remain with all the functions it has now.
To fund my work, I robbed my father.
But the money wasn't his, and he shot himself.

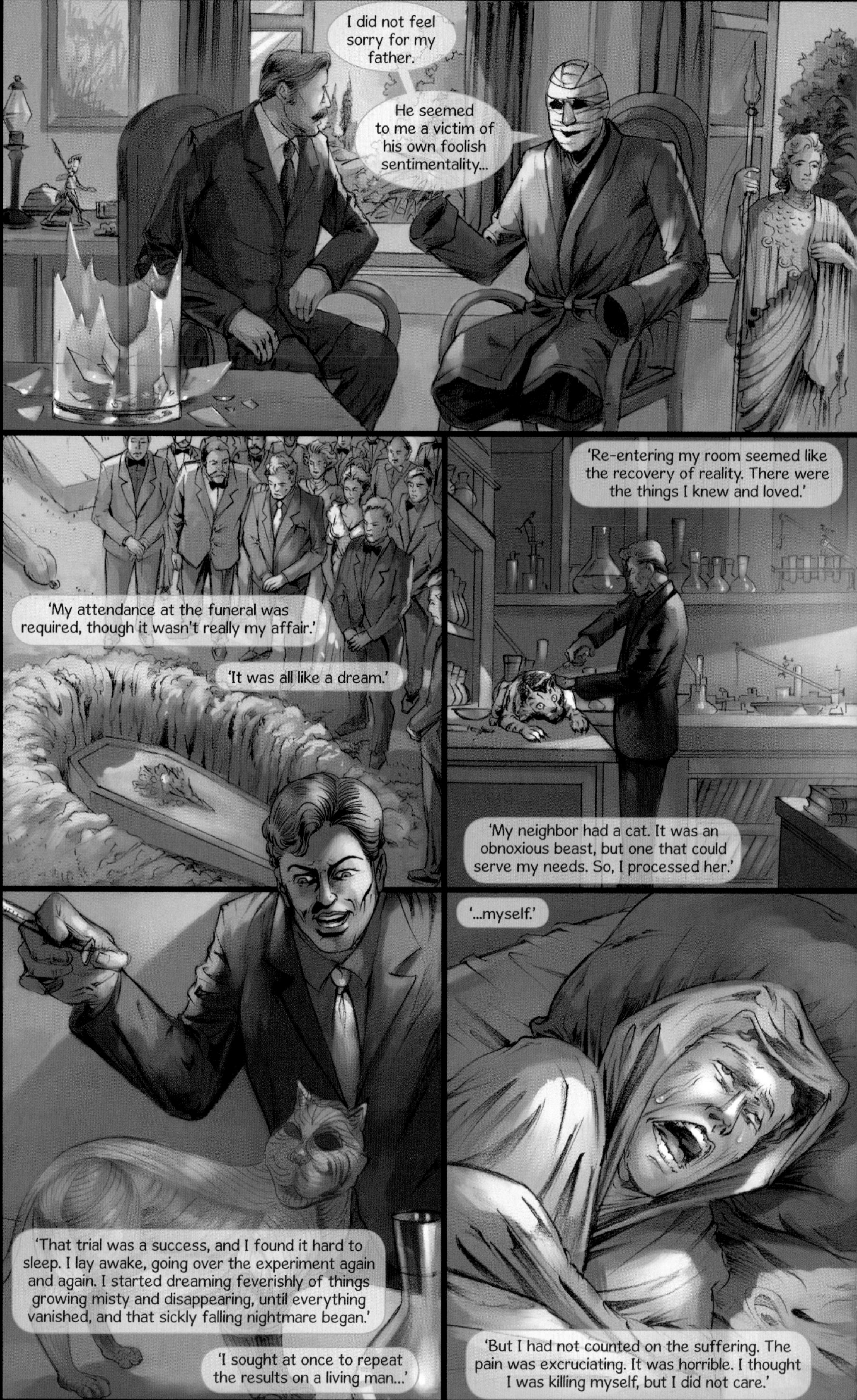

I did not feel sorry for my father.
He seemed to me a victim of his own foolish sentimentality...
'My attendance at the funeral was required, though it wasn't really my affair.'
'It was all like a dream.'
'Re-entering my room seemed like the recovery of reality. There were the things I knew and loved.'
'My neighbor had a cat. It was an obnoxious beast, but one that could serve my needs. So, I processed her.'
'That trial was a success, and I found it hard to sleep. I lay awake, going over the experiment again and again. I started dreaming feverishly of things growing misty and disappearing, until everything vanished, and that sickly falling nightmare began.'
'I sought at once to repeat the results on a living man...'
'...myself.'
'But I had not counted on the suffering. The pain was excruciating. It was horrible. I thought I was killing myself, but I did not care.'

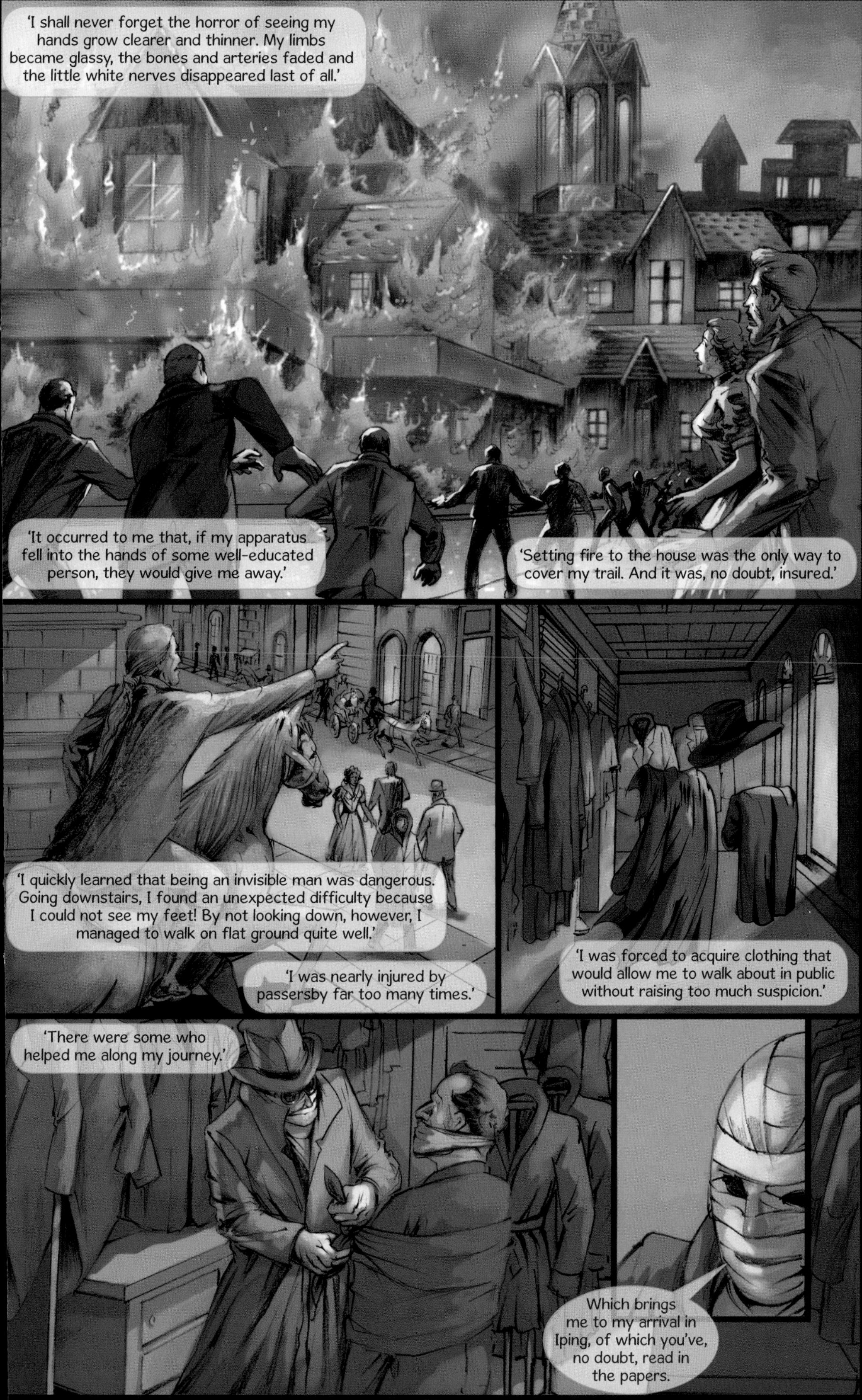

'I shall never forget the horror of seeing my hands grow clearer and thinner. My limbs became glassy, the bones and arteries faded and the little white nerves disappeared last of all.'
'It occurred to me that, if my apparatus fell into the hands of some well-educated person, they would give me away.'
'Setting fire to the house was the only way to cover my trail. And it was, no doubt, insured.'
'I quickly learned that being an invisible man was dangerous. Going downstairs, I found an unexpected difficulty because I could not see my feet! By not looking down, however, I managed to walk on flat ground quite well.'
'I was nearly injured by passersby far too many times.'
'I was forced to acquire clothing that would allow me to walk about in public without raising too much suspicion.'
'There were some who helped me along my journey.'
Which brings me to my arrival in Iping, of which you've, no doubt, read in the papers.

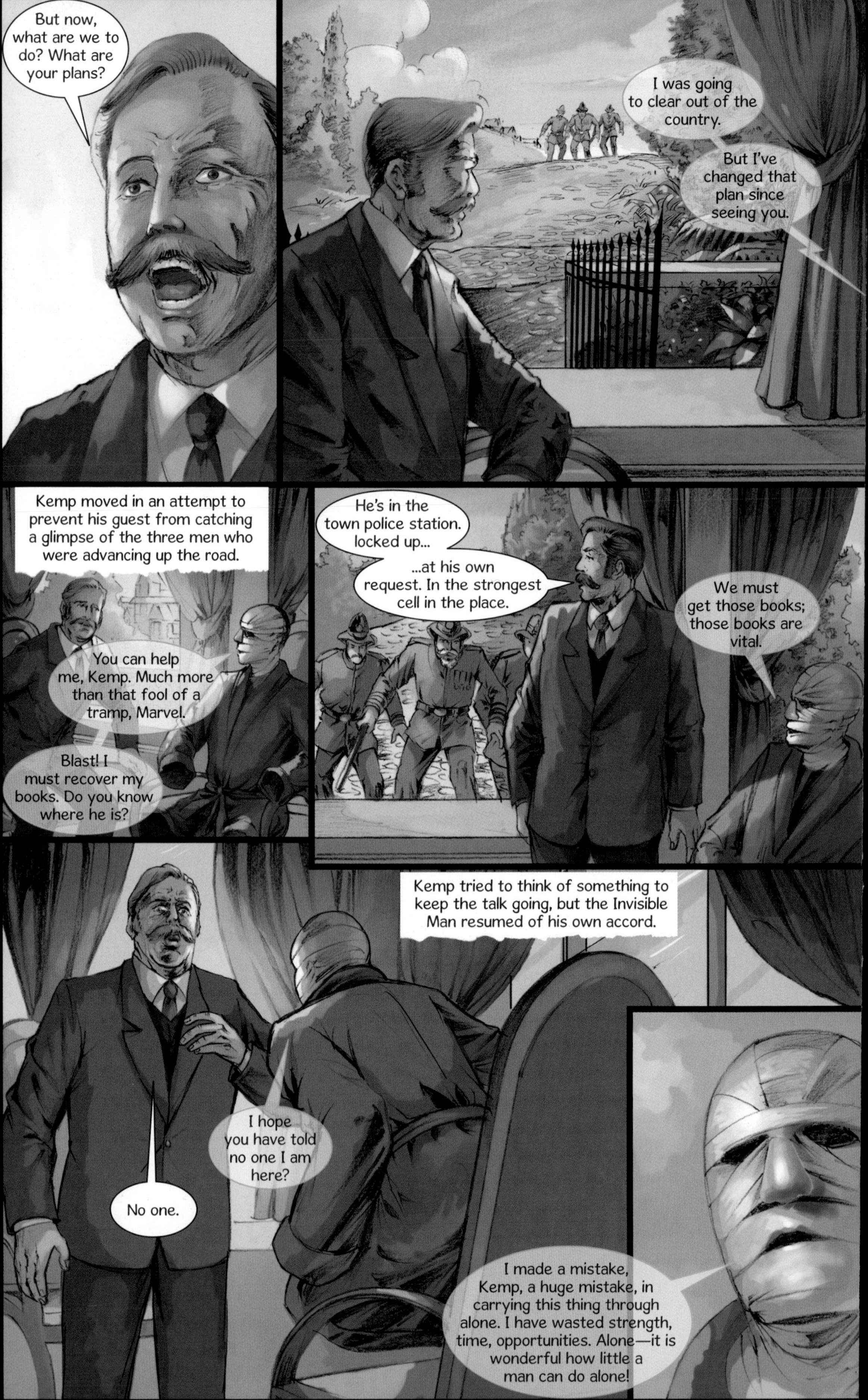
But now, what are we to do? What are your plans?
I was going to clear out of the country.
But I've changed that plan since seeing you.
Kemp moved in an attempt to prevent his guest from catching a glimpse of the three men who were advancing up the road.
You can help me, Kemp. Much more than that fool of a tramp, Marvel.
Blast! I must recover my books. Do you know where he is?
He's in the town police station. locked up...
...at his own request. In the strongest cell in the place.
We must get those books; those books are vital.
Kemp tried to think of something to keep the talk going, but the Invisible Man resumed of his own accord.
I hope you have told no one I am here?
No one.
I made a mistake, Kemp, a huge mistake, in carrying this thing through alone. I have wasted strength, time, opportunities. Alone—it is wonderful how little a man can do alone!

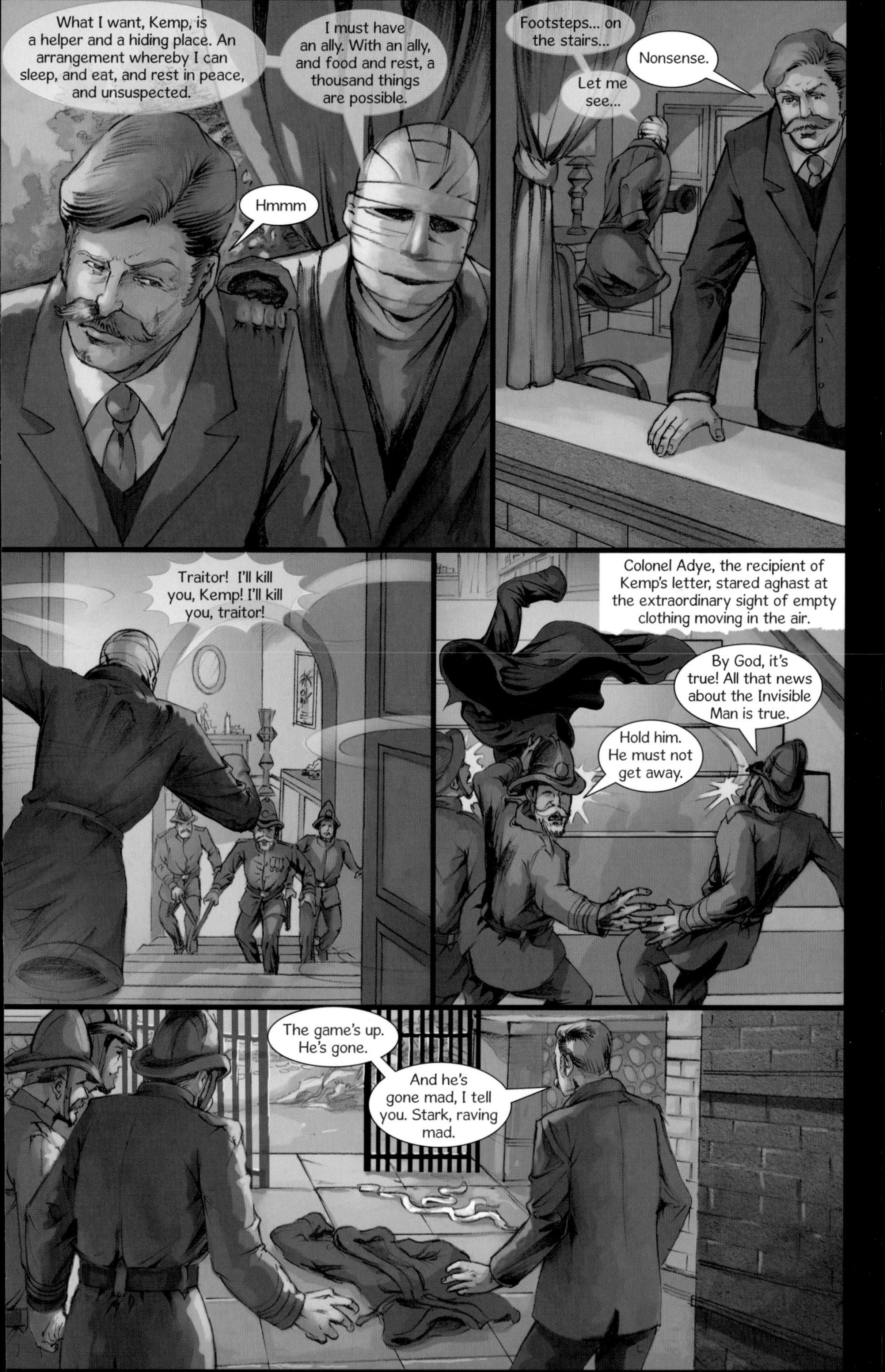
What I want, Kemp, is a helper and a hiding place. An arrangement whereby I can sleep, and eat, and rest in peace, and unsuspected.
I must have an ally. With an ally, and food and rest, a thousand things are possible.
Hmmm
Footsteps... on the stairs...
Let me see...
Nonsense.
Traitor! I'll kill you, Kemp! I'll kill you, traitor!
Colonel Adye, the recipient of Kemp's letter, stared aghast at the extraordinary sight of empty clothing moving in the air.
By God, it's true! All that news about the Invisible Man is true.
Hold him. He must not get away.
The game's up. He's gone.
And he's gone mad, I tell you. Stark, raving mad.

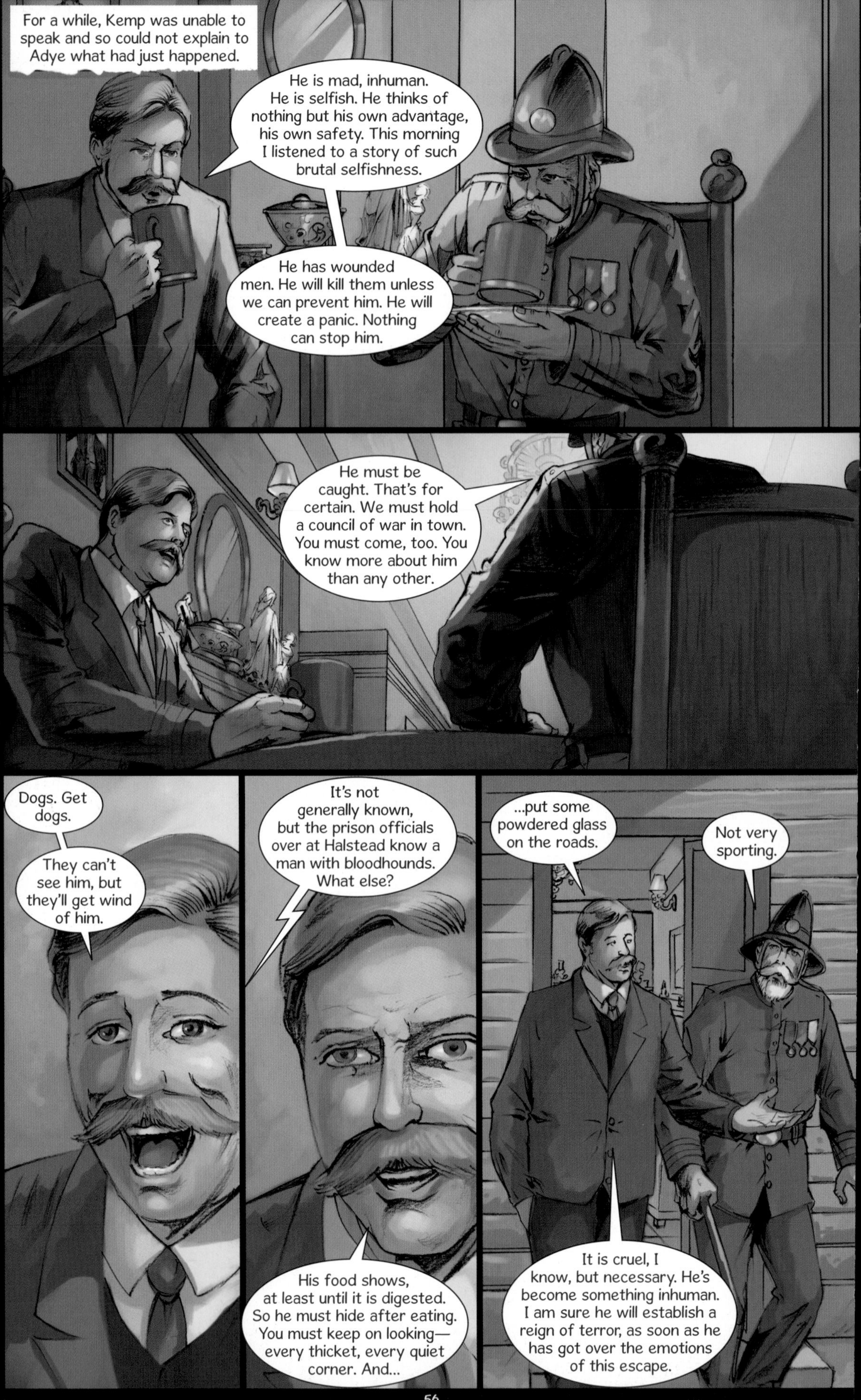
For a while, Kemp was unable to speak and so could not explain to Adye what had just happened.
He is mad, inhuman. He is selfish. He thinks of nothing but his own advantage, his own safety. This morning I listened to a story of such brutal selfishness.
He has wounded men. He will kill them unless we can prevent him. He will create a panic. Nothing can stop him.
He must be caught. That's for certain. We must hold a council of war in town. You must come, too. You know more about him than any other.
Dogs. Get dogs.
They can't see him, but they'll get wind of him.
It's not generally known, but the prison officials over at Halstead know a man with bloodhounds. What else?
His food shows, at least until it is digested. So he must hide after eating. You must keep on looking— every thicket, every quiet corner. And...
...put some powdered glass on the roads.
Not very sporting.
It is cruel, I know, but necessary. He's become something inhuman. I am sure he will establish a reign of terror, as soon as he has got over the emotions of this escape.

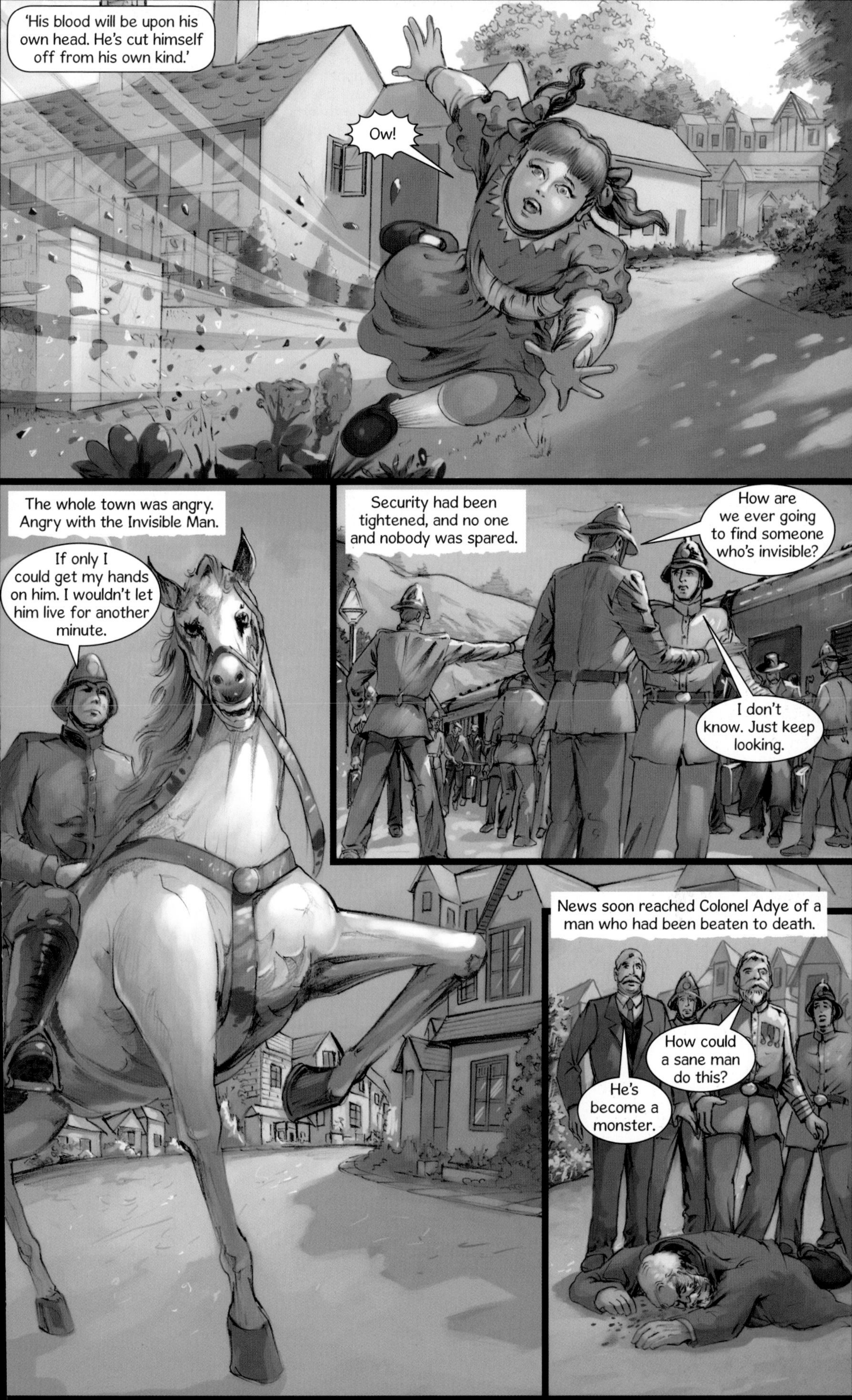
'His blood will be upon his own head. He's cut himself off from his own kind.'
Ow!
The whole town was angry. Angry with the Invisible Man.
If only I could get my hands on him. I wouldn't let him live for another minute.
Security had been tightened, and no one and nobody was spared.
How are we ever going to find someone who's invisible?
I don't know. Just keep looking.
News soon reached Colonel Adye of a man who had been beaten to death.
How could a sane man do this?
He's become a monster.

He appears to have been beaten with a rod from a fence.

Yes. We must increase our efforts to catch Griffin. Or I fear this won't be the last of the killings.

Some time later, Adye and Kemp walked back to Kemp's house.

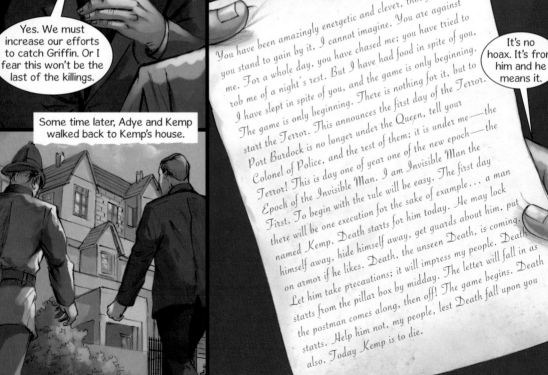

The moment Kemp entered, the housekeeper gave him a letter.

It's no hoax. It's from him and he means it.

You have been amazingly energetic and clever, though what you stand to gain by it, I cannot imagine. You are against me. For a whole day, you have chased me; you have tried to rob me of a night's rest. But I have had food in spite of you, I have slept in spite of you, and the game is only beginning. The game is only beginning. There is nothing for it, but to start the Terror. This announces the first day of the Terror. Port Burdock is no longer under the Queen, tell your Colonel of Police, and the rest of them; it is under me——the Terror! This is day one of year one of the new epoch——the Epoch of the Invisible Man. I am Invisible Man the First. To begin with the rule will be easy. The first day there will be one execution for the sake of example... a man named Kemp. Death starts for him today. He may lock himself away, hide himself away, get guards about him, put on armor if he likes. Death, the unseen Death, is coming. Let him take precautions; it will impress my people. Death starts from the pillar box by midday. The game begins. Death starts when the postman comes along, then off! The letter will fall in as the postman comes along, then off! The game begins. Death starts. Help him not, my people, lest Death fall upon you also. Today Kemp is to die.

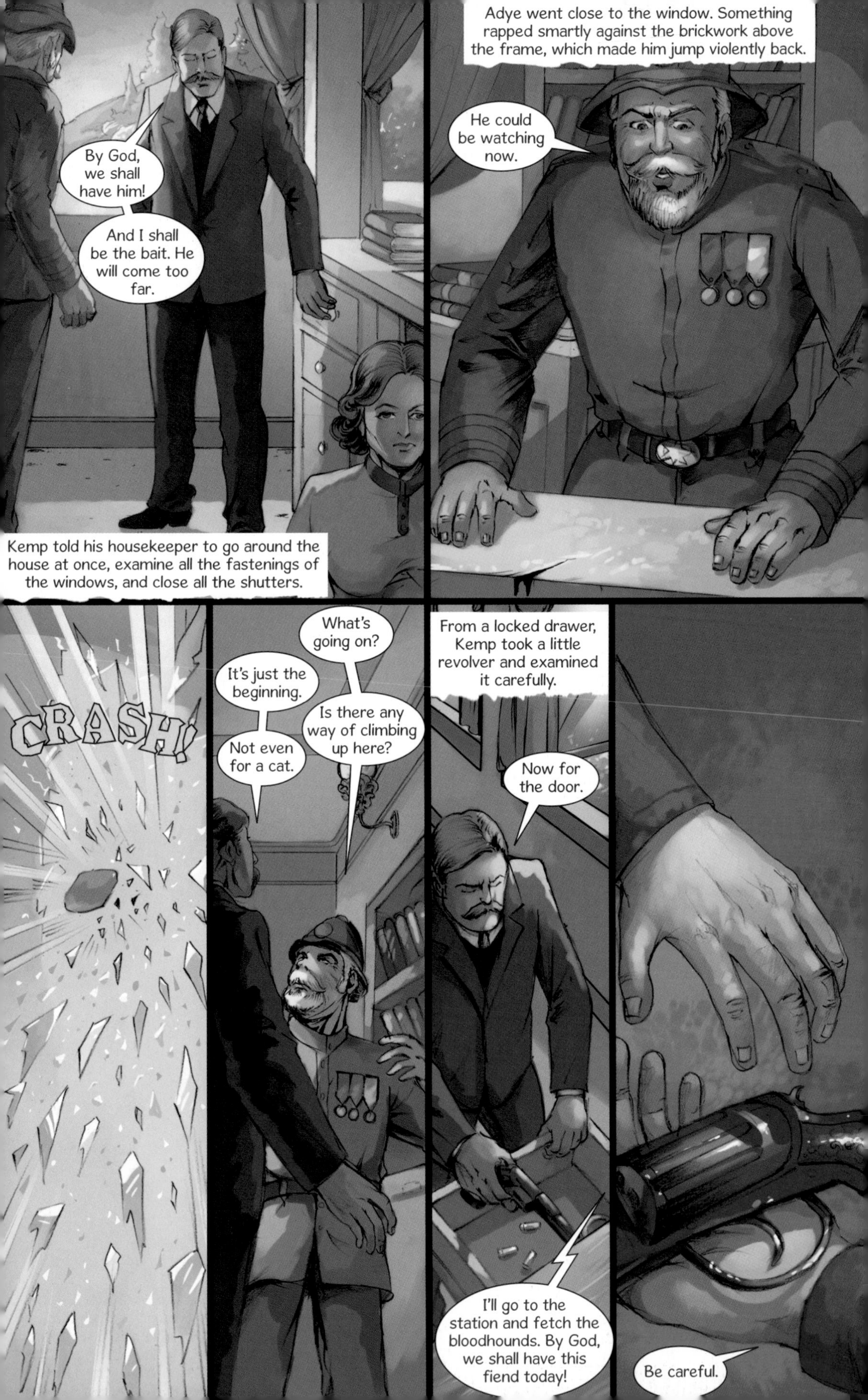
By God, we shall have him!
And I shall be the bait. He will come too far.
Kemp told his housekeeper to go around the house at once, examine all the fastenings of the windows, and close all the shutters.
Adye went close to the window. Something rapped smartly against the brickwork above the frame, which made him jump violently back.
He could be watching now.
CRASH!
What's going on?
It's just the beginning.
Is there any way of climbing up here?
Not even for a cat.
From a locked drawer, Kemp took a little revolver and examined it carefully.
Now for the door.
I'll go to the station and fetch the bloodhounds. By God, we shall have this fiend today!
Be careful.

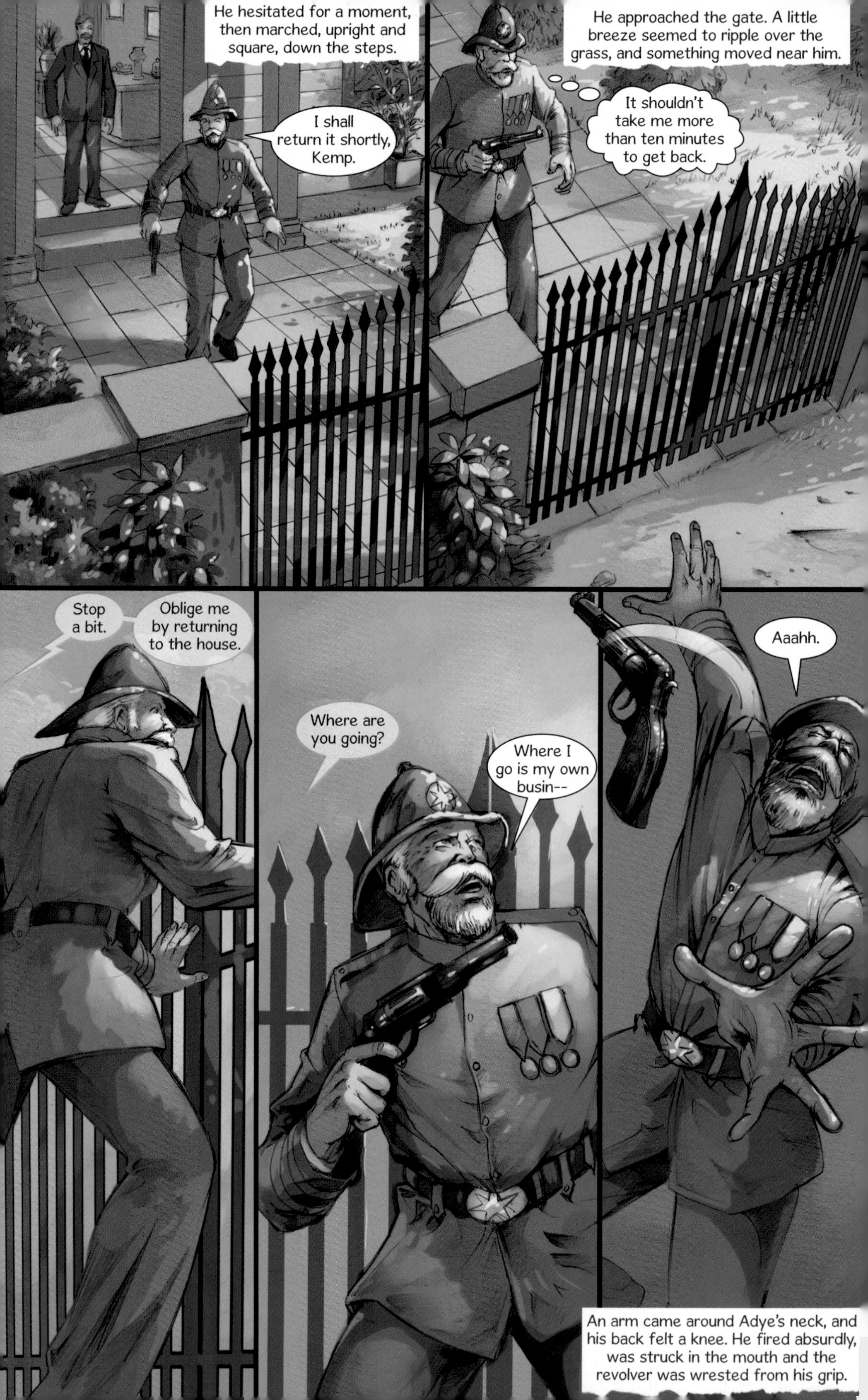
He hesitated for a moment, then marched, upright and square, down the steps.
I shall return it shortly, Kemp.
He approached the gate. A little breeze seemed to ripple over the grass, and something moved near him.
It shouldn't take me more than ten minutes to get back.
Stop a bit.
Oblige me by returning to the house.
Where are you going?
Where I go is my own busin--
Aaahh.
An arm came around Adye's neck, and his back felt a knee. He fired absurdly, was struck in the mouth and the revolver was wrested from his grip.

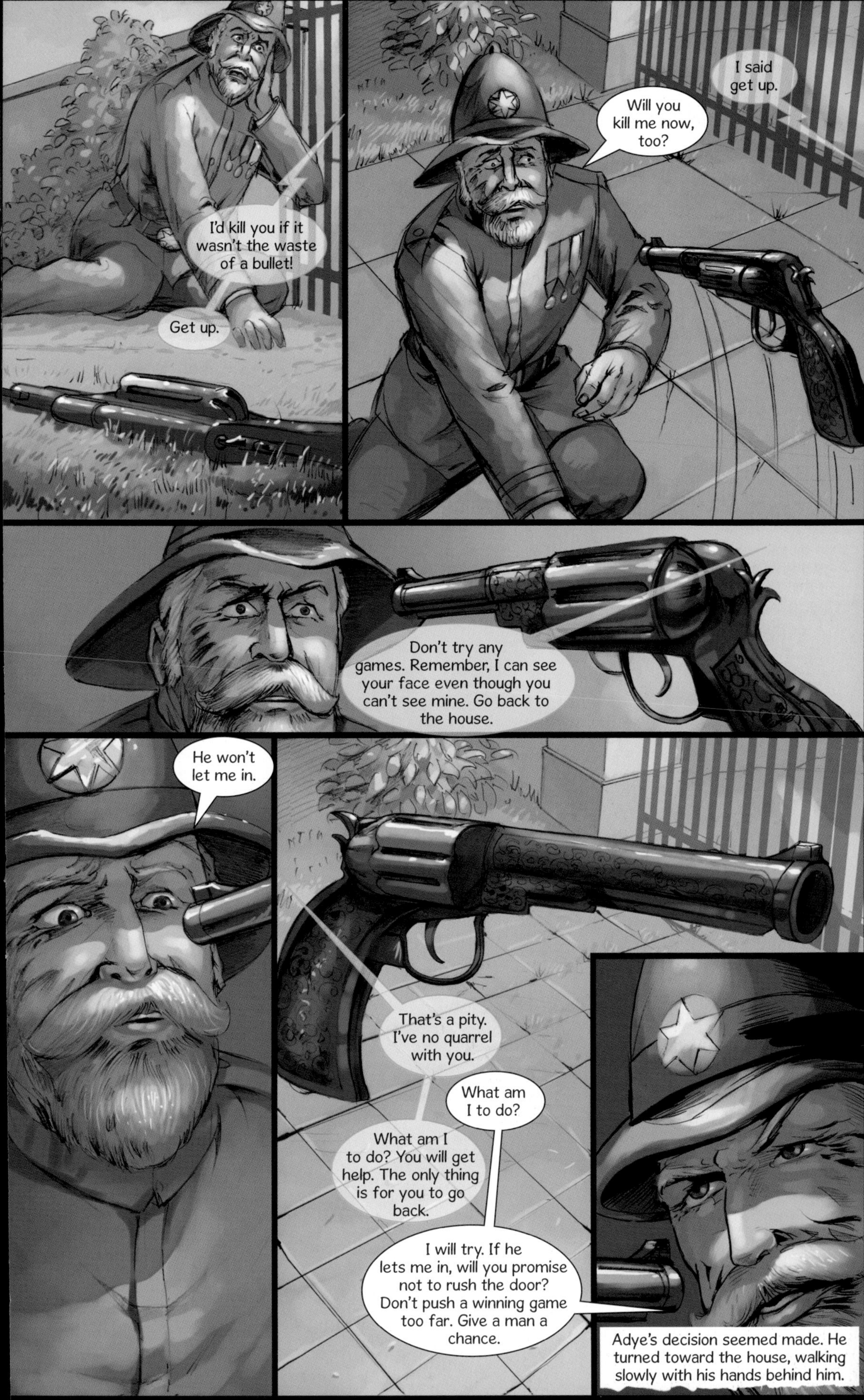
I'd kill you if it wasn't the waste of a bullet!
Get up.
Will you kill me now, too?
I said get up.
Don't try any games. Remember, I can see your face even though you can't see mine. Go back to the house.
He won't let me in.
That's a pity. I've no quarrel with you.
What am I to do?
What am I to do? You will get help. The only thing is for you to go back.
I will try. If he lets me in, will you promise not to rush the door?
Don't push a winning game too far. Give a man a chance.
Adye's decision seemed made. He turned toward the house, walking slowly with his hands behind him.

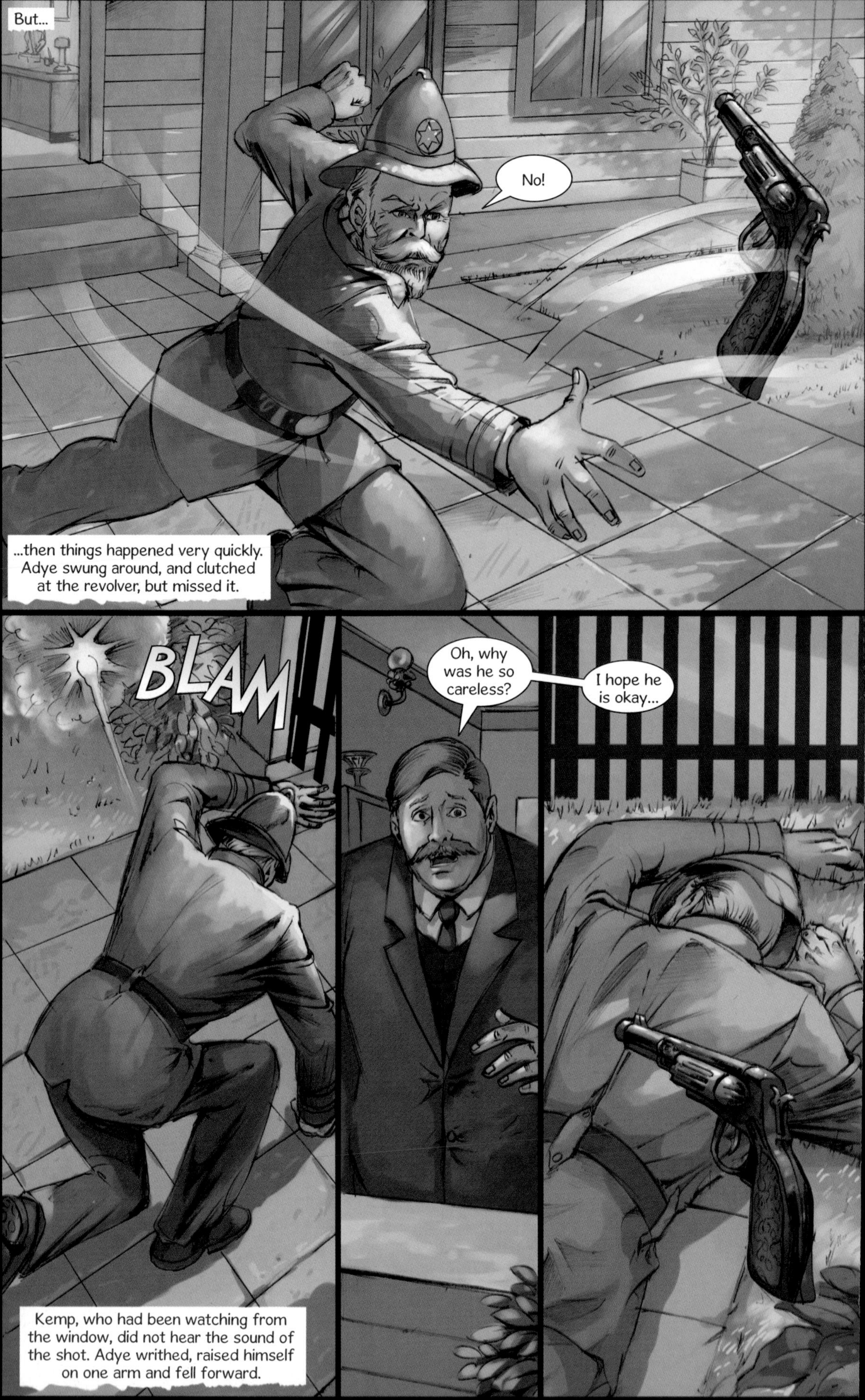
But...
No!
...then things happened very quickly. Adye swung around, and clutched at the revolver, but missed it.
BLAM
Oh, why was he so careless?
I hope he is okay...
Kemp, who had been watching from the window, did not hear the sound of the shot. Adye writhed, raised himself on one arm and fell forward.

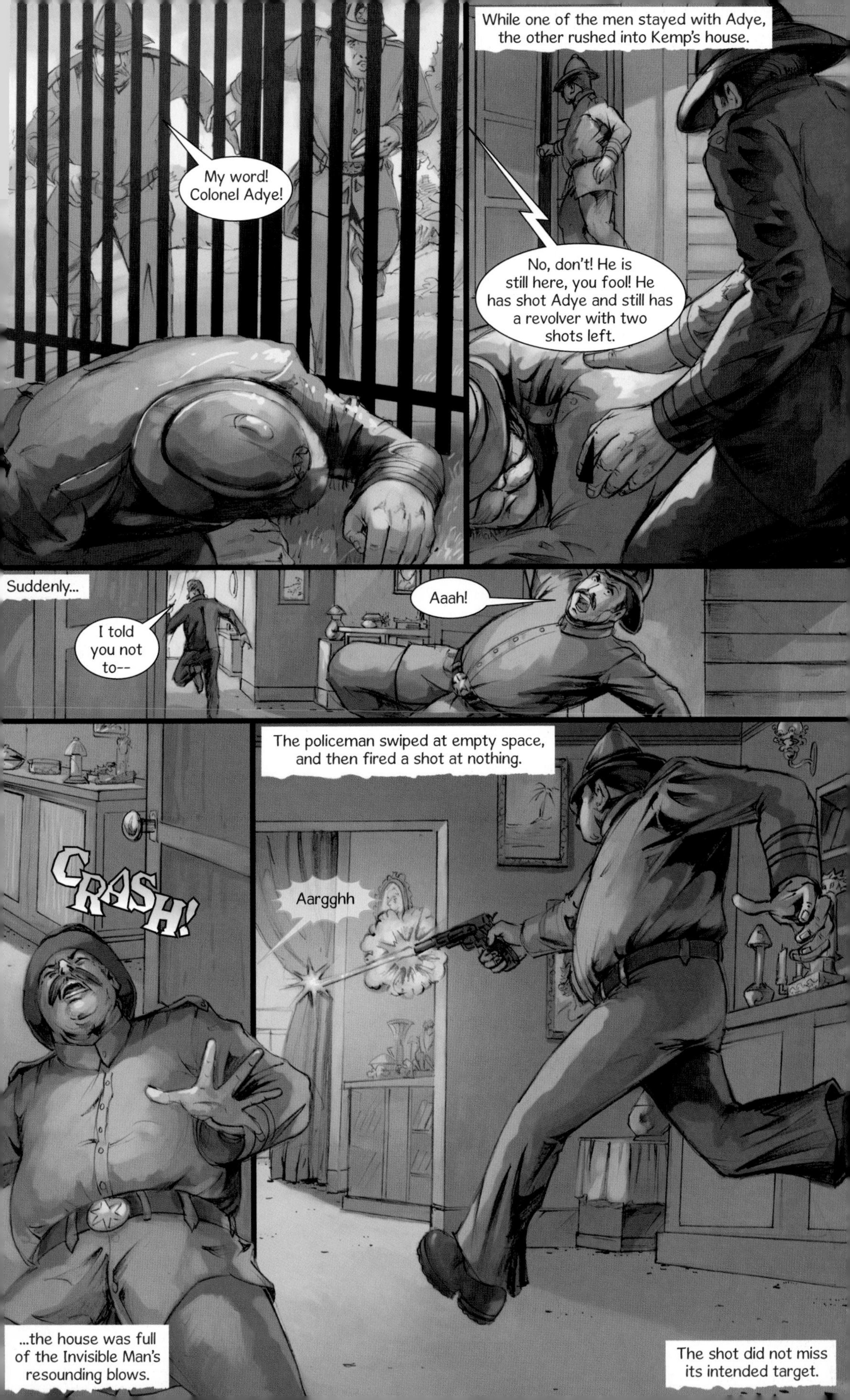
My word! Colonel Adye!
While one of the men stayed with Adye, the other rushed into Kemp's house.
No, don't! He is still here, you fool! He has shot Adye and still has a revolver with two shots left.
Suddenly...
I told you not to--
Aaah!
CRASH!
...the house was full of the Invisible Man's resounding blows.
The policeman swiped at empty space, and then fired a shot at nothing.
Aargghh
The shot did not miss its intended target.

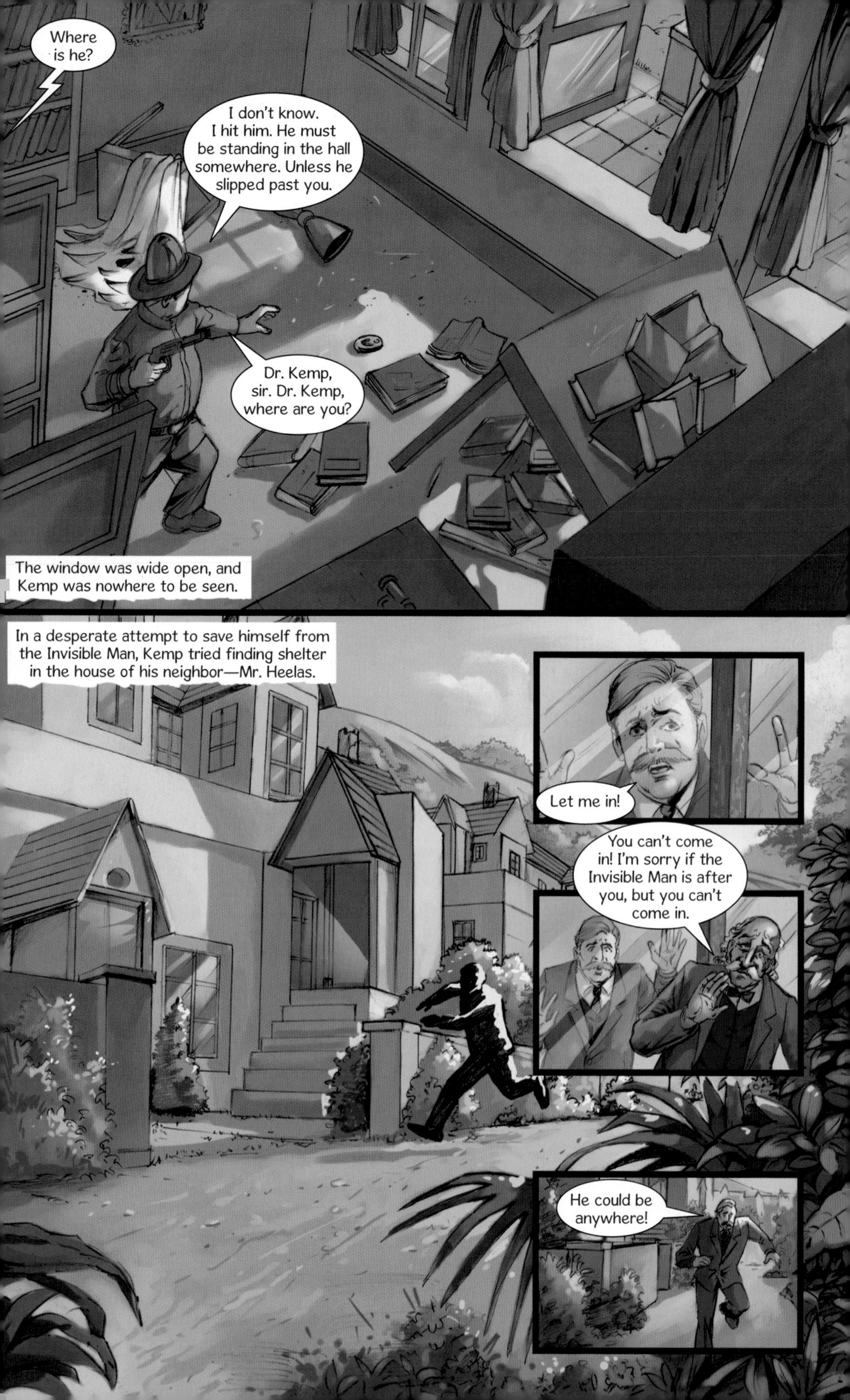
Where is he?
I don't know. I hit him. He must be standing in the hall somewhere. Unless he slipped past you.
Dr. Kemp, sir. Dr. Kemp, where are you?
The window was wide open, and Kemp was nowhere to be seen.
In a desperate attempt to save himself from the Invisible Man, Kemp tried finding shelter in the house of his neighbor—Mr. Heelas.
Let me in!
You can't come in! I'm sorry if the Invisible Man is after you, but you can't come in.
He could be anywhere!

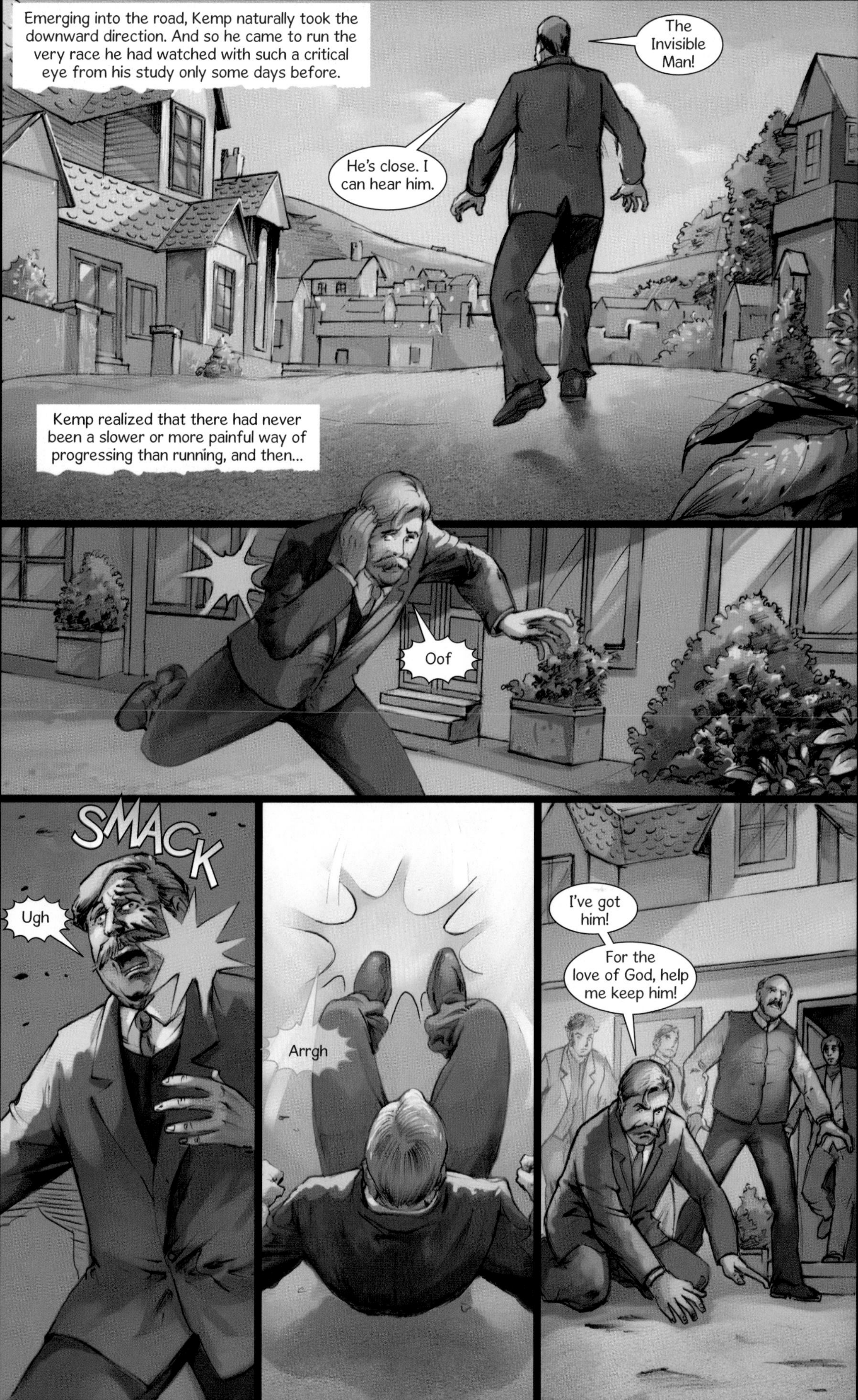

Emerging into the road, Kemp naturally took the downward direction. And so he came to run the very race he had watched with such a critical eye from his study only some days before.
The Invisible Man!
He's close. I can hear him.
Kemp realized that there had never been a slower or more painful way of progressing than running, and then...
Oof
SMACK
Ugh
Arrgh
I've got him!
For the love of God, help me keep him!

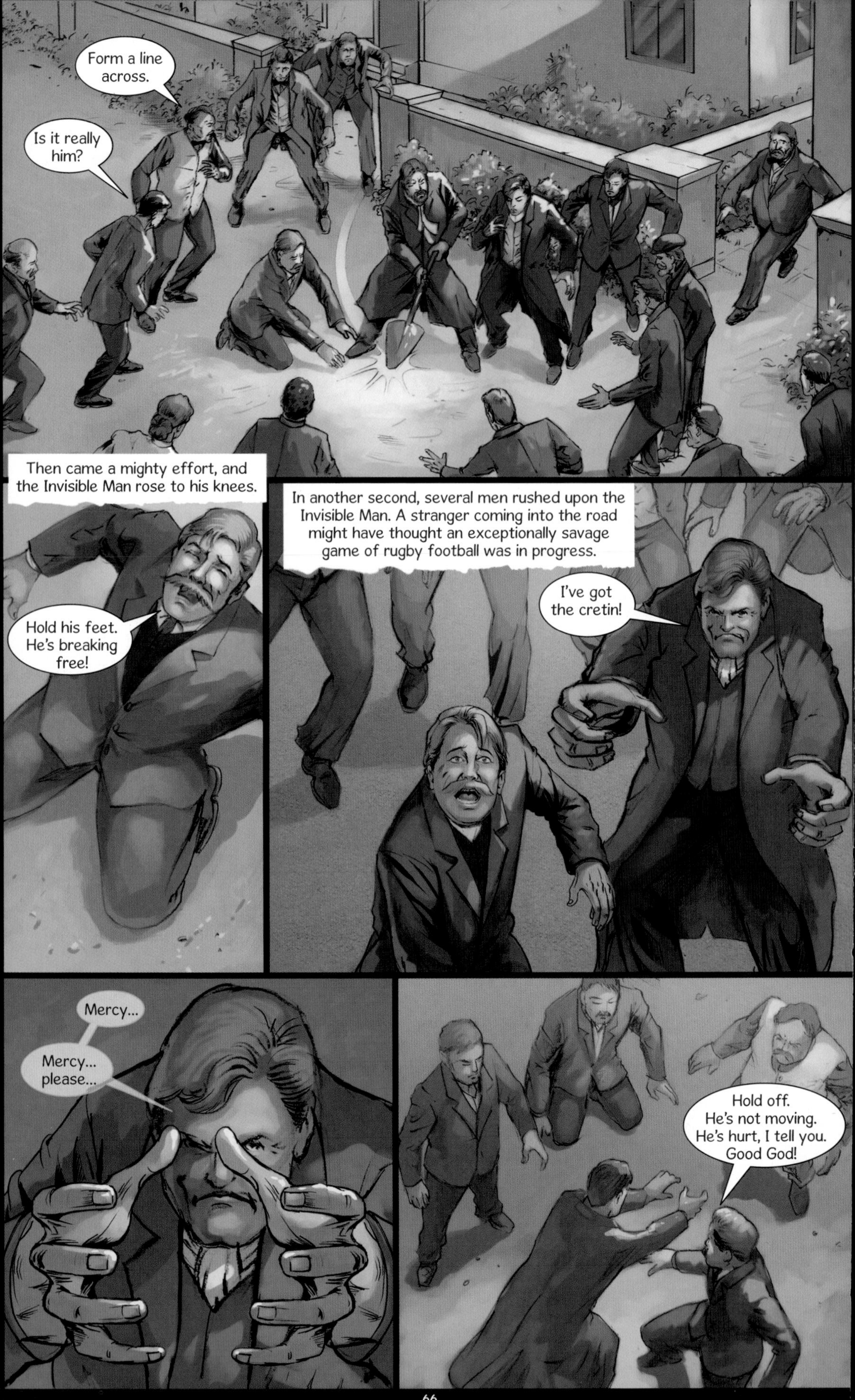
Form a line across.
Is it really him?
Then came a mighty effort, and the Invisible Man rose to his knees.
Hold his feet. He's breaking free!
In another second, several men rushed upon the Invisible Man. A stranger coming into the road might have thought an exceptionally savage game of rugby football was in progress.
I've got the cretin!
Mercy...
Mercy... please...
Hold off. He's not moving. He's hurt, I tell you. Good God!

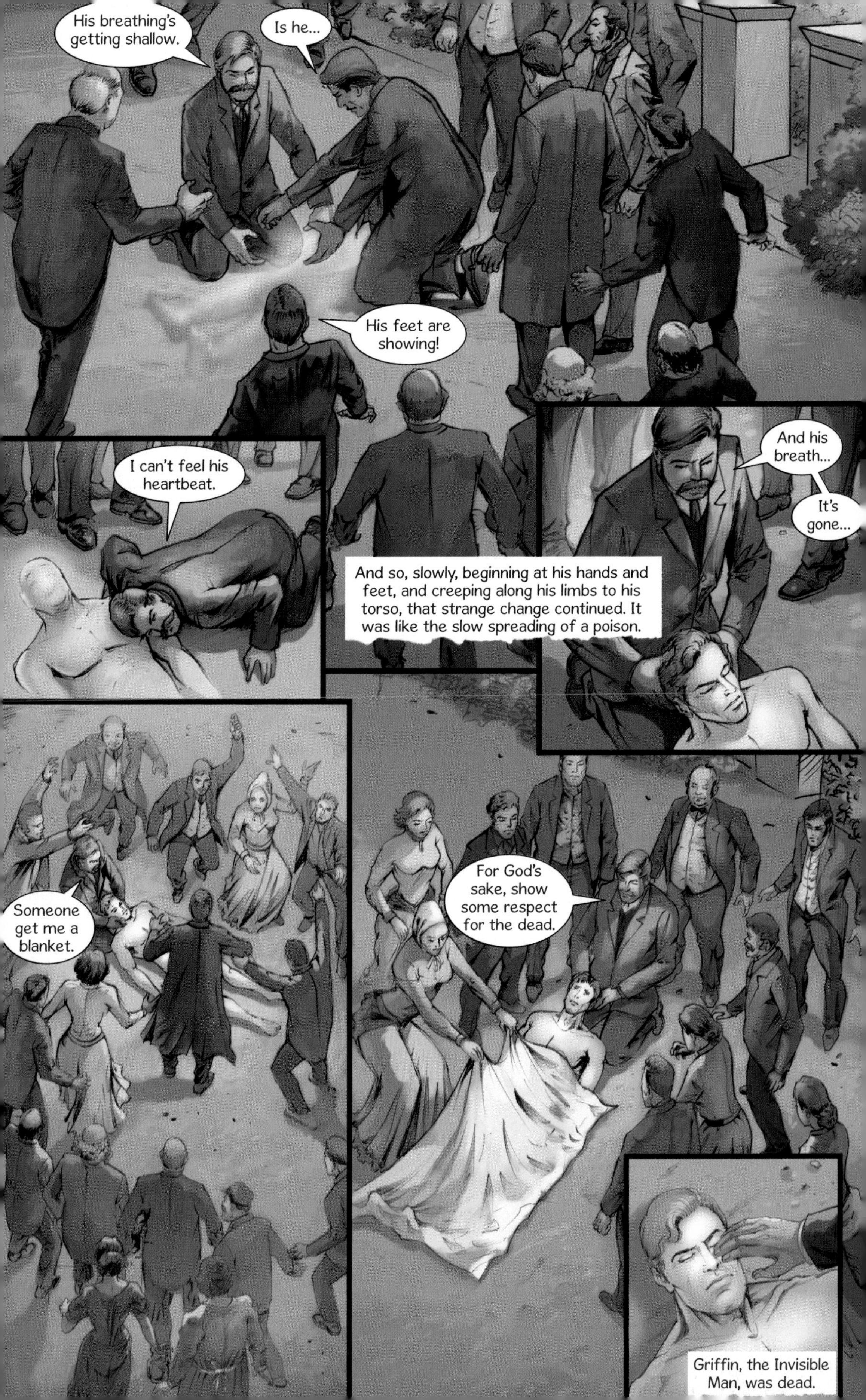
His breathing's getting shallow.
Is he...
His feet are showing!
I can't feel his heartbeat.
And so, slowly, beginning at his hands and feet, and creeping along his limbs to his torso, that strange change continued. It was like the slow spreading of a poison.
And his breath...
It's gone...
Someone get me a blanket.
For God's sake, show some respect for the dead.
Griffin, the Invisible Man, was dead.

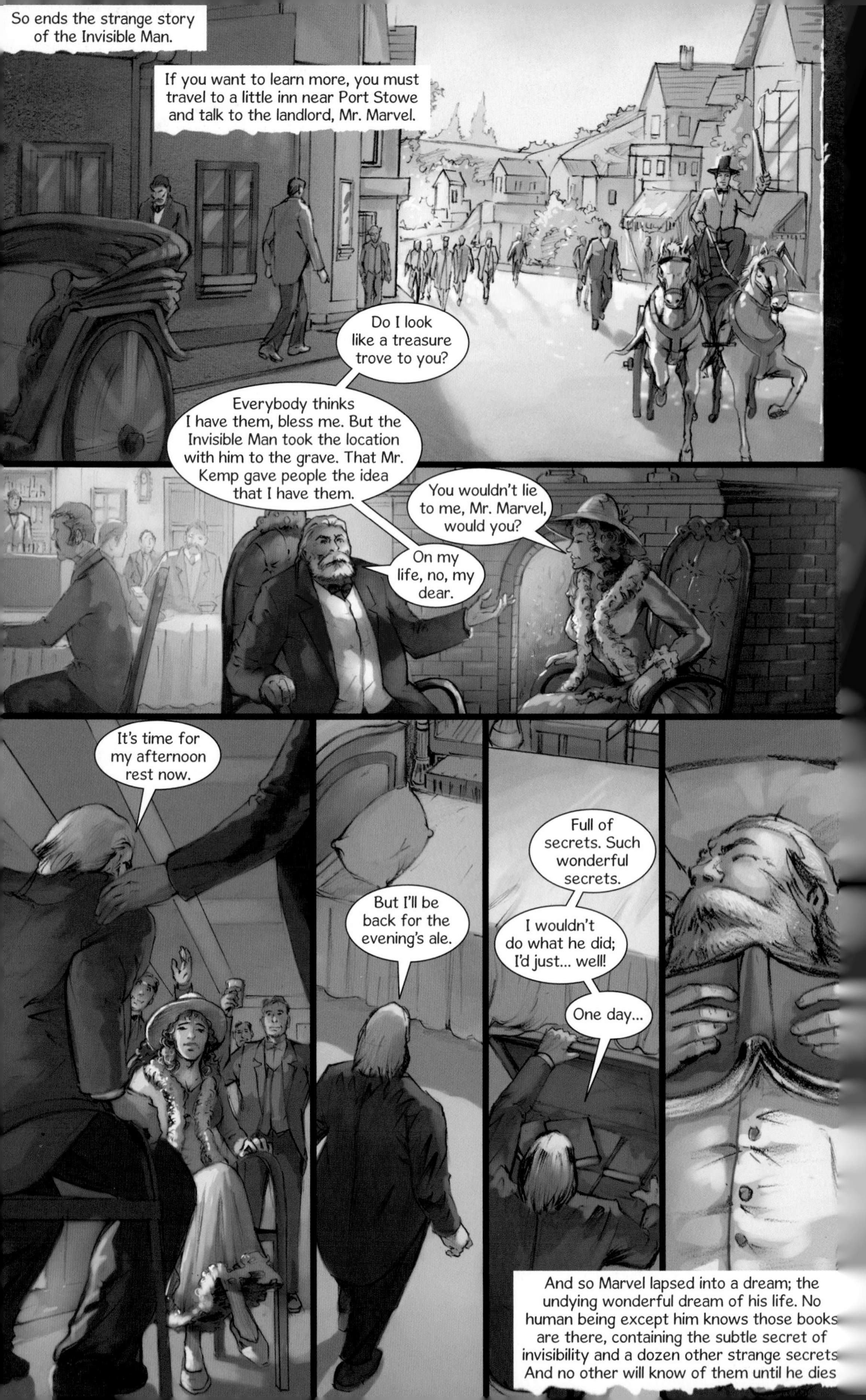
So ends the strange story of the Invisible Man.
If you want to learn more, you must travel to a little inn near Port Stowe and talk to the landlord, Mr. Marvel.
Do I look like a treasure trove to you?
Everybody thinks I have them, bless me. But the Invisible Man took the location with him to the grave. That Mr. Kemp gave people the idea that I have them.
You wouldn't lie to me, Mr. Marvel, would you?
On my life, no, my dear.
It's time for my afternoon rest now.
But I'll be back for the evening's ale.
Full of secrets. Such wonderful secrets.
I wouldn't do what he did; I'd just... well!
One day...
And so Marvel lapsed into a dream; the undying wonderful dream of his life. No human being except him knows those books are there, containing the subtle secret of invisibility and a dozen other strange secrets And no other will know of them until he dies

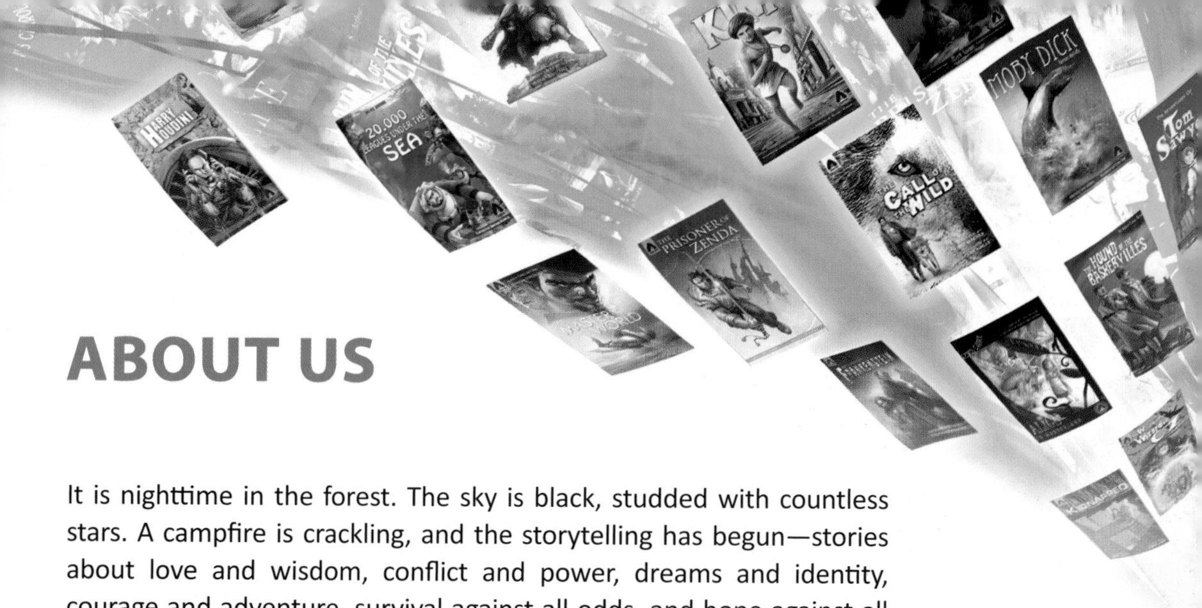
HARRY HOUDINI
20,000 LEAGUES UNDER THE SEA
MOBY DICK
THE CALL OF THE WILD
THE PRISONER OF ZENDA
THE HOUND OF THE BASKERVILLES
Tom Sawyer

ABOUT US

It is nighttime in the forest. The sky is black, studded with countless stars. A campfire is crackling, and the storytelling has begun—stories about love and wisdom, conflict and power, dreams and identity, courage and adventure, survival against all odds, and hope against all hope. In the warm, cheerful radiance of the campfire, the storyteller's audience is captivated, as in a trance. Even the trees and the earth and the animals of the forest seem to have fallen silent, bewitched.

Inspired by this enduring relationship between a campfire and gripping storytelling, we bring you four series of *Campfire Graphic Novels*:

Our *Classic* tales adapt timeless literature from some of the greatest writers ever.

Our *Mythology* series features epics, myths and legends from around the world, tales that transport readers to lands of mystery and magic.

Our *Biography* titles bring to life remarkable and inspiring figures from history.

Our *Original* line showcases brand new characters and stories from some of today's most talented graphic novelists and illustrators.

We hope you will gather around our campfire and discover the fascinating stories and characters inside our books.

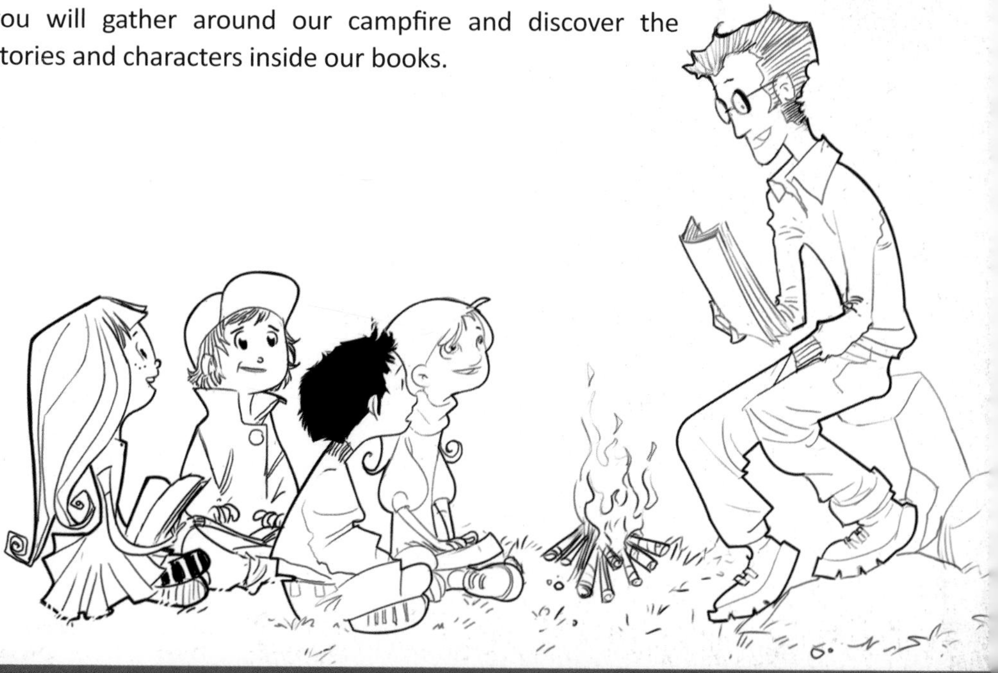

CAMPFIRE™

AMAZING ALBINOS

In this story, the Invisible Man is 'almost an albino'. Let's find out more about albinism and how it affects creatures from the animal kingdom.

WHAT IS ALBINISM?
The color we see in living creatures is caused by a pigment called melanin. An albino has no melanin in its body which makes it completely white.

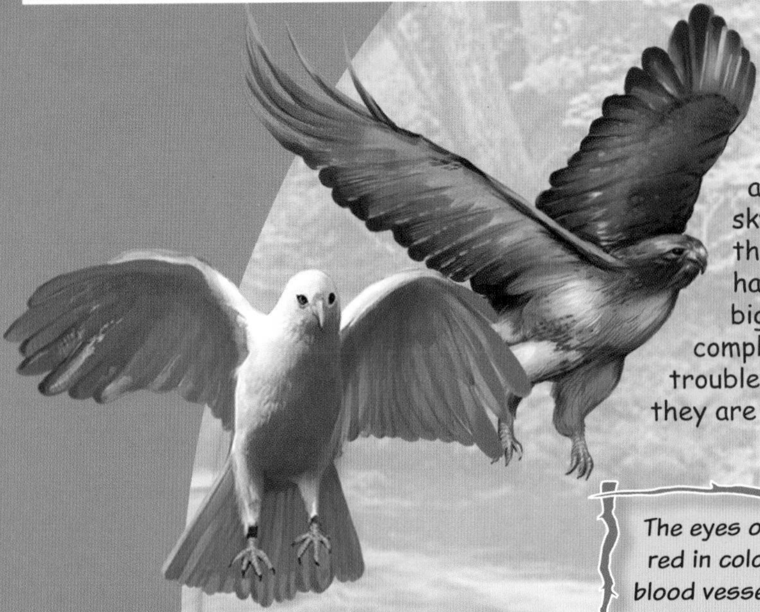

HAWKS

Hawks are huge birds with clawed feet which eat small animals and fly high in the sky. Albino hawks, while having the same stature as other hawks, could be mistaken for big doves as their feathers are completely white. They are often troubled by other hawks because they are so different from the rest.

The eyes of albino animals are often red in color. This is because the red blood vessels of the retina show right through their transparent eyes.

ALLIGATORS

Alligators are large meat-eating reptiles which mostly live in fresh water, swamps, and lakes. Albino alligators are forced to remain in shaded areas as the harmful rays of the sun can burn or even kill them. White Diamond, a famous albino alligator, was born in Louisiana in the U.S.A. and is now a star of a traveling reptile show called Land der Reptilien.

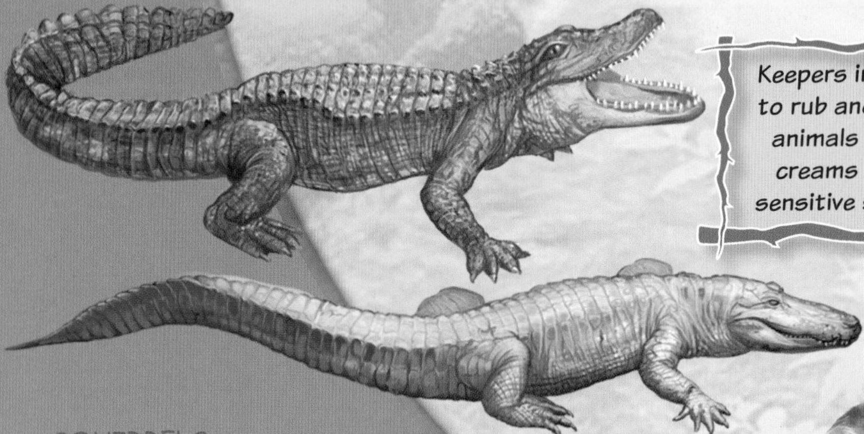

Keepers in zoos often have to rub and cover the albino animals with lotions and creams to protect their sensitive skin from the sun.

SQUIRRELS

You have probably seen these furry creatures in woods and parks, scampering for nuts and berries. Olney, a city in the U.S.A., is known as the 'White Squirrel Capital of the World', and is home to the world's largest known albino-squirrel colony! The people of this city are so proud of the creatures that even the police department's badge has a picture of a white squirrel on it.

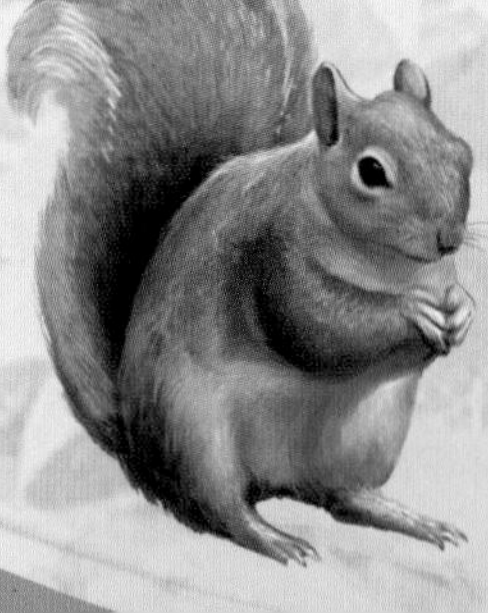

HEDGEHOGS

Albino hedgehogs, like the rest of their species, live under hedges and eat insects. They are very rare and you are unlikely to recognize one. This is because their white fur gets dirty from all the scuttling they do under the hedges and they end up looking like normal brown hedgehogs.

KANGAROOS

Kangaroos are most commonly seen hopping across the grassy plains of Australia. An interesting fact is that there are no known albino kangaroos in the wild—most of them live in zoos where they are often the star attraction.

Did you know that albino animals are seen as messengers from God in many Native American cultures? It is considered extremely lucky to see one.

PENGUINS

These lovable black and white flightless birds spend most of their time in the water and only come to land to rear their young. Albino penguins are not very different in appearance from other penguins; they are just lighter in color. Bristol Zoo, in England, was home to Snowdrop, Britain's first albino penguin. Snowdrop was hatched at the zoo in 2002, but died in 2004.

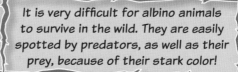

It is very difficult for albino animals to survive in the wild. They are easily spotted by predators, as well as their prey, because of their stark color!

ALSO AVAILABLE FROM
CAMPFIRE GRAPHIC NOVELS

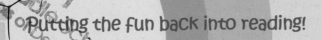

Putting the fun back into reading!

Explore the latest from Campfire at
www.campfire.co.in